Hot in the City

CASSANDRA O'LEARY

Contents

Chocolate Truffle Kiss

A Romantic Comedy Novelette

Cassandra O'Leary

MONDAY

Your eyes meet mine, then retreat
Softness behind glass
Let me break your barriers

The poem on the blackboard enticed her to enter. Just like every day. Each afternoon when Beth escaped work for a few minutes' peace. Someone jostled her shoulder as they opened the door to her left and a waft of rich, aromatic deliciousness teased her senses. Melbourne's finest single origin fair trade caffeine goodness and other indulgent treats.

But first, a new mini-poem greeted her. Today's was sweet – a tentative love story. The poems added a sparkling glint of spring sunshine to her days, assisted by delicious coffee and the even more delicious-looking man behind the counter.

She let her imagination run rampant, standing on the footpath, rubbing her icy fingertips together to ward off the chill breeze whipping through the city street. She read the poem again, the distinctive cursive script etched on the A-frame board adding an artistic touch.

The poems were written for her. It was him, he was the poet. 'Hot café guy'. Or on her more creative days, the Dragon Master, after his distinctive forearm tattoo. But she knew his real name after so many months. The barista, Samuel. She imagined he watched her the way she watched him, quietly, inconspicuously enjoying the view.

Ridiculous. A proper nutjob. As if he'd notice me, average in every way. Average height and weight, maybe a tad skinny, weak chai latte skin, light blue eyes. Long, strawberry blonde curls were her only noticeable feature. And she was old . . . thirty-eight was a dinosaur in today's online insta-dating scene.

Palm pressing into cold glass, the heavy wooden framed

door opened, and she stepped into comforting warmth. She looked down at the intricate square of mosaic tiles beneath her feet, a creative welcome mat, as the old-fashioned bell above the door jingled. Raising her head, her gaze locked on him.

Samuel, dark and brooding, held court behind the stream-lined Art Deco espresso machine, chatting with two older women. Beth wasn't the only customer to fall under his spell.

"Really, Sam-u-elle?" asked the plumper of the two. "A new coffee for me to try? But I like mine hot, dark and sweet, just like my men."

Samuel whispered something too low for Beth to hear, then shook his head, treating both women to a cheeky wink. They soon left, laughing like schoolgirls, the older grey-haired lady fanning her face theatrically.

Beth approached the counter, aware of his every move-ment. Samuel steamed milk under the chrome nozzle, his biceps exposed by a tight black t-shirt. She was a dirty old woman, ogling his strong jaw shadowed with stubble, and the tattooed dragons and Celtic style crosses intertwined down his muscular, tanned arms.

She had to be ten years older. God, maybe fifteen. A *cougar*, much as she hated to admit it. If not already a crazy cat lady.

He turned and flicked his long black hair, dark eyes alight when he smiled. Bubbles of frothy pleasure rose in her belly. He'd noticed her.

"Beth." He smiled again, that smile could melt chocolate from one hundred paces. "I'm just making your usual latte. I'll bring it over to you."

"Thanks, Samuel." She ducked behind the espresso machine and rolled her eyes at herself. Did she have to sound so breathy and fan-girlish whenever she spoke to him?

She crossed the checkerboard black and white tiles, then dumped her oversize leather handbag on her usual table, grabbing her favourite notebook and pen from the inner pocket. The city street view was great for people-watching. Capturing whatever details popped into her mind, feeding her hobby as a writer. The words appeared in her head and poured onto the page like liquid dreams. She was never short of inspiration here.

Samuel stalked across the tiles towards her, silent and graceful as a big cat. But she was aware of him. Oh, so aware. Her skin prickled at the back of her neck and goose bumps raced down her arms as he neared. He placed the red glossy cup and saucer on the scrubbed pine table. There was an elegant heart and swirl in the coffee foam. And a delectable chocolate truffle on the side.

"Enjoy." His smile beamed like shimmering sunlight through the leadlight windows by the café door. She blinked slowly, soaking up his attention. Once he'd turned away, she jotted the shimmering description down. That was damned good.

Why did inspiration hit so often when he was near?

The bell jingled, almost distracting her from the drool-worthy sight of Samuel walking away, his slim black jeans fitting sublimely. A group of university students entered, chattering over tablet computers and library books as they settled into one of the red leather booths. A couple of the girls batted eyelashes in Samuel's direction, but he didn't seem to notice.

Before long, she had a page of notes and her half-hour break was up. Sooner than she'd like, as usual. Draining the dregs of her coffee, she made the most of the last morsel of her truffle. Licking her fingers, she glanced up to find Samuel watching. Great, he probably thought she had disgusting table manners now.

Except, the way he'd watched her with glittering black diamond eyes said something else entirely. He looked ... hungry.

Whoa. She didn't need that look fanning the flames of her hot and steamy thoughts.

Fossicking in her purse, she struck gold. She counted out enough coins to cover her bill and stacked them neatly in the middle of the table. With a little extra as a tip, for him. Her muse.

TUESDAY

> *Divine indulgence*
> *Awaits the brave*
> *Chocolate, coffee and you*
> *All I crave*

He lowered his head towards hers, dipping his chin. Everything inside her tightened, heated. Cinnamon and manly spice, strong arms wrapped around her, his dark eyes flashing.

"Beth!" Beth's old friend arrived in her usual full-on style, slamming the door and flouncing across the room.

Beth snapped her head up, rudely awakened from her daydream. Was her face completely red? She hoped no-one one could hear her heartbeat thumping like a jackhammer. She had been sitting at her usual table, still pondering today's poem.

Chocolate, coffee and you. All I crave.

She could say those words to Samuel. If she were brave. Then the daydream had taken on a life of its own.

Jenny took a seat like she was perching on a throne, the queen of Beth's table, dramatically arranging designer shopping bags beside her chair. Beth's glance slipped to Samuel where he leaned on the counter. His raised eyebrow gave a hint of his thoughts. He probably thought she was a loner with no friends. How could he know she wanted him all to herself? Samuel was her secret indulgence.

Her love-life was officially extinct. That's exactly what the coffee catch-up with her oldest friend was supposed to be about – kick-starting Beth's apparently dormant sex drive. So here they were. Jenny talked her into meeting here, and now had grand plans to enrol Beth in a singles club or some such scheme, to get her back on the dating scene.

A year had gone by since Beth's divorce, and everyone agreed it was time. Everyone suddenly tried to set her up with all the 'suitable', single, fifty-ish men they could find. Whether she liked it or not. When they last chatted on the phone, Jenny had informed Beth that she would "dry up" if she didn't get some action soon. Little did Jenny know that Beth's sex drive switched automatically to hyperdrive whenever she glanced Samuel's way.

Beth had made an exception for Jenny, inviting her to meet at her favourite café. Jenny was her childhood friend who she hardly saw, since Jenny had moved interstate with a high-powered job and equally high-powered husband.

Samuel watched their table, openly, checking out Jenny from coiffed head to perfectly shod toe. Beth should have stood up for herself, should never have brought Jenny to her favourite café. Her friend was lithe and effortlessly elegant with the perfect blonde hairdo and immaculate black suit and heels. If Samuel wanted an older woman, he'd probably choose someone like Jenny.

Beth glanced down at her own outfit. Her offbeat style, combat boots and a second-hand 1970s floral dress today, turned heads for the wrong reasons. She didn't really care anymore. Not usually. The ad agency where she worked as a copywriter was happy with alternative gear. She wore what she liked, what felt comfortable. That was one good thing about getting older – she was more confident in her own style and in her own skin. Except when a man she desired was watching another woman right in front of her.

"Beth, darling, look at you!" Jenny leaned over and air-kissed her cheek. "Your dress is so cute. And your hair is to die for, as always." Jenny turned and snapped her fingers at Samuel as if he was her personal serving-boy.

Beth's cheeks warmed. "Jenny, behave." Her warning tone apparently fell on deaf ears.

"Why? Is that him? Hot café guy?" Jenny's voice boomed across the café. Then her icy blue eyes evaluated him, thoroughly. Head to toe, all the good places in between. "He's certainly hot. And he wants you too, I can tell."

Beth's cheeks heated. Her whole body was tinder dry, about to burst into flame with the flick of a struck match. Her gaze snapped across to the counter to find Samuel staring. Really, properly staring, as if he could see straight into her soul. Or at least into her dirtiest fantasies. As if he heard her thunderous heart beating from across the room and finally understood the pathetic, unrequited crush she nurtured deep inside.

He quickly turned away, busily stacking coffee mugs. Jenny didn't notice the silent exchange and tottered over to the counter to place her order.

After a few minutes of boasting about her new home (on Jenny's part), Beth was beginning to wonder if she and Jenny had anything in common anymore. Samuel delivered Jenny's coffee to their table with a furtive glance in Beth's direction. A quick but steamy glance.

Was she wrong, or was there definite smoulder in those coal ember eyes? And there she went. *Whoosh*. On fire.

"Where's my chocolate truffle? I've heard they're divine." The superior note in Jenny's voice made Beth's stomach churn. Was her friend always so condescending?

Samuel shrugged, then walked over to another table of customers.

"Only for Beth. I see." Jenny laughed loudly. "Never mind."

Beth cringed inside, then downed her coffee in a single gulp, mind reeling.

Did Samuel like her? Chewing her divine truffle, she thought it through. Any attraction on his part seemed unlikely. He could have any hot young chick. Half of the students who came into the café asked him out. Girls and guys. Although, she'd never noticed him accept any of their invitations.

He was probably taken. She'd bet he had some super-model girlfriend ready to give up her jet-setting lifestyle to have his babies. Or maybe he was a private person, an intro-vert like herself.

The conversation with Jenny lurched along. Beth prepared herself, sitting up straighter, then told her friend something important.

"I've got some news. A couple of my short stories are about to be published. There's a book launch coming up and everything." It was exciting, something Beth had worked long and hard to achieve. Her heart fluttered a little in her chest, finally having the chance to tell someone.

"Really? Some of your little stories? After all these years? Well, good on you. That's so... fun." Jenny touched Beth's arm, giving her a little pat.

Beth's heart sank like a stone in a cold bucket of water. Apparently, Jenny didn't see the point, if a book wouldn't sell a million copies. Her eyes stung, but she wouldn't cry. She'd had enough of tears the last few years.

Beth endured a few more minutes of mindless chatter, then Jenny left in a flurry of air kisses and *dah-lings*, with a promise to meet soon. Beth didn't commit to anything.

Then, Samuel's gaze was on her again. Time slowed to the pace of thick caramel syrup dripping off the back of a spoon as Samuel sauntered across the floor to her table.

She stood and met his eyes, tilted her head upwards. They

were only centimetres apart, a hand's breadth. It would be so easy to reach out and touch him.

"Did your friend like the place?" Samuel asked.

"I think so." She paused to suck in much needed oxygen. Her heart wobbled now he was here, standing so close. Making her want things. "Sorry she's a bit loud. A bit much in general, sometimes."

"Don't apologise. I wasn't offended." He paused and looked her straight in the eye, but only for a second. Then his gaze dropped to his feet. "Did she like today's poem?"

"I don't know. But I did, I always do. Who writes them?"

Samuel studied the floor, then took a deep breath that made his chest expand. He peeked up underneath long black eyelashes. "It's a secret. The poet prefers it that way."

Before she could respond, or even find her voice, he'd picked up her bag and passed it to her. Standing so close, she inhaled the scent of his skin – woody, intense, spiced with cinnamon. Their fingers brushed, quickly. Softly. Only a moment. But somehow it was one of life's big moments. At least it was for her.

Her heart stopped mid-thump, her blood flowed slowly, languidly, her eyelids hit half-mast. Heat flooded her belly and settled between her thighs. Her whole body screamed, 'Take me to bed!' but he was already gone.

Back behind the counter, making coffee, serving customers. He barely noticed when she dropped her money by the register and left.

WEDNESDAY

A touch
A taste
A tease
A torment

When she entered the café that afternoon, the bell rang with its jaunty jingle. But there was another pretty sound. Samuel's voice floated and echoed across the tiled room towards her. An old Michael Hutchence song about precious hearts and two worlds colliding.

Heaven on a stick.

His voice was liquid sugar, sweet and smooth, but overflowing with pure sensuality. He had it. Charisma, sex appeal, animal magnetism. Whatever it was, that some singers and movie stars had. Samuel had it and a bit. And *it* hit her right in the ovaries.

A voice like that, combined with his body, it wasn't fair. It was like he was there just to taunt and tempt her.

She sidled up to the counter, achingly aware of every inch of her skin as he hit a high note. "That song's a bit old for you to remember, isn't it?"

Samuel shook his head, wiping down the countertop at the same time. "It's a classic. How old do you think I am exactly?"

"I don't know, twenty-four, twenty-five, maybe?"

He smiled, flashing white teeth and a killer dimple. "I'm glad I've still got it. I'm thirty-two."

Her mouth formed a silent 'O'. Only six years younger. She shouldn't think about it. Shouldn't get her hopes up. He was still too young. But not embarrassingly young. Perfect for a woman who'd always liked younger men. Until a certain ex-husband proved to be a boy in a man's body, juvenile and self-centred.

"Still, young and handsome and with a stunning voice. Not old and decrepit like me."

"Thanks, but ... decrepit?" His gaze strolled a lazy path from her eyes to her nude lips, detoured at the low neckline of her black t-shirt and down her red mini skirt to her exposed legs. "You look absolutely *fine* from where I'm standing."

Oh, holy hell. She was about to spontaneously combust right in front of him. Somehow she found her voice, even if it was breathier than usual. That was pretty breathy. "Thanks, that's um, nice to know."

Nice. *Nice?* She deserved his laughter, but damn if his low, throaty chuckle didn't just continue the chain reaction inside her. He'd said he found her attractive, hadn't he? Something like that. She backed away and headed for the refuge of her usual table. Putting distance between them.

She sat and crossed her legs to one side, conscious suddenly that he might be watching her. Grabbing her notebook and pen, she settled down to write. Swirling thoughts of kissing, touching—a gorgeous man singing—derailed her current story. But the ideas were good, worth saving for later.

A hint of something in the air, the scent of rich, warm coffee or vibrant, hot man, then his thighs. *Dammit.* His denim-clad thighs were right there beside her, firm and sumptuous enough to bite.

Samuel was at her side, delivering her coffee and truffle. He placed them on the table and as he shifted his hand, brushed his thumb against her knuckles. His touch was warm, sending tingles every which way.

She trembled so violently she drew a jagged line right across her page and dropped her pen. It clattered against the tiled floor.

"Sorry. Oh, man. I didn't mean to startle you." He crouched down and picked it up. She could only stare.

Their eyes were level. Her fingertips twitched, wanting to reach out and stroke her hand across his jaw, press her lips to his. Of course, she didn't move. He placed the pen gently on her notebook.

Then he trilled at her, or rather, his jeans did. She blinked, regaining her senses. He grabbed his phone from his back pocket and stood, mouthing the word 'sorry' again as he took the call and walked away.

She shouldn't have listened, but she couldn't write. Her heart pounded too hard and her skin felt two sizes too small. Sipping her coffee, she tried not to overhear his conversation. She just didn't try very hard. There were only a couple of other customers in the café so late in the afternoon and from where he stood behind the espresso machine, his voice carried loud and clear.

"Talia, sweetheart, I asked you to call me tonight."

Sweetheart? Her stomach clenched. He did have a girlfriend. *Of course he does, genius!*

"I know, the time difference is a killer. That's exactly the problem."

Time difference. So, she was somewhere overseas. Probably on holiday or at a work conference. What did the beautiful Talia do for a job? No doubt she was beautiful. Probably a supermodel, or a brain surgeon. A glamorous supermodel brain surgeon.

"I know, I know. The opportunity of a lifetime. I get it."

Beth risked a glance at Samuel and found him already looking at her. His eyes snared her in a trap, pulling her down into his sexy lair. She didn't mind being lured in. Not one bit. Then he turned away, raking a hand through his luscious black hair. She let out a staggered breath. The moment, the connection, lost. She ducked her head, taking a big bite of her truffle.

"I just wanted to be a part of it. Not stuck on the other side of the world."

Sipping her latte, she choked on a gulp that went down the wrong way. Was there trouble in paradise with the beautiful Talia?

"Talk later. Yep, me too."

Him too. What? Loved her? Missed her? Wanted to tie her up in his man-cave and shag her senseless so she'd never leave home again?

Her hand tightened on her coffee cup. It didn't matter. He

was off-limits. She should never have entertained the idea. She finished her treat in a gloomy fog that not even chocolate could dissipate.

She left her money on the table, her hand shaking. She didn't want him to see that. No way she'd approach the counter or talk to him again. But he walked by as she was nearing the door. He stopped and folded those muscular arms across his chest, causing the dragon's wings to take flight across his forearm.

"I have a confession. You asked yesterday about the poems." He hesitated, biting his full lower lip. "I write them. Songs too. Some people inspire me, you know?" His smile tipped up on one side, letting his dimple out to play. Melting her insides.

He couldn't mean her, could he? Was she his inspiration, as he was hers? That would be too perfect. Her life and perfect didn't fit together.

And yet. . . she hadn't given up. She wanted to find that someone special. Her ex-husband Pete hadn't been her one true love, but she'd known that going in with eyes wide open. Luckily, she'd learned from the experience. She wouldn't settle again.

"I write too." Taking a deep breath, she squeezed her eyes shut for a second. Then the words tumbled out. "Short stories mostly. Love stories, fantasy too."

"I know. I mean, I didn't spy on your work, but I always see you writing in your notebook. You look like you enjoy it."

"A couple of my stories are being published soon. In an anthology." She ducked her head so her curly hair fell over her face. Why did she tell him that? If he was anything like Pete, or Jenny, he'd soon put her in her place for getting excited over her small achievement. Then he'd be no-one special, no-one to fantasise about.

"That's fantastic! You'll have to let me know when the book comes out. I'll be first in line for your autograph."

She lifted her head and beamed all over him. Of course, he'd be the only person in her life who'd get excited for her. Somehow, she'd known he'd understand and be happy for her. He was lovely like that. *Lovely but taken.* Her annoying conscience spoke up, whooshing the breath out of her lungs. She held onto the door handle for support.

She had to go. Had to get back to work, but more importantly, she needed to get away from Samuel. He had a girlfriend, and it wasn't cool to flirt with him any longer. She'd never break up someone else's relationship to get what she wanted. Unlike her charming ex-husband who saw their neighbour's pretty young wife and moved in for the kill.

"See you tomorrow, Beth." Samuel nodded and pushed open the door for her.

She couldn't answer. Her tight smile fell away as she stepped outside, her good mood left behind.

Tomorrow. She didn't think she could face him tomorrow.

Thursday

What to do?
About you
The future, us
I wonder, do you feel it intensely too?

Beth considered staying away. She considered it carefully for about one millisecond. Her feet travelled in that direction anyway, before her brain could click into gear. When she read the poem, standing in the blustery wind, she knew she'd never stay away. Not when he was there, writing poems, making glorious coffee and plying her with chocolate that fuelled her daydreams.

Maybe today's poem was about his girlfriend on the other side of the world. How could she know? Her chest constricted at the idea of *her* poems belonging to another woman. But it was sweet and touching. She loved reading them and now she knew Samuel wrote them, she loved them all the more. She'd savour them, as if they were chocolate truffles.

Pushing the café door, she jingle-jangled loudly. The door was stuck. Probably the wet weather making the wooden frame swell. Melbourne's sudden turn from spring to winter weather didn't bother her much, although she struggled with her umbrella and the door as sprinkles of light rain fell on her hair and jacket.

The glass beneath her palm gave way and she stumbled inside.

Samuel stood there, holding the door, looking all huge and hot and handsome. She sighed, straightening, admiring him in his tight, blood red t-shirt.

"Hello." His voice was extra low and rumbly. Stormy, with a chance of thunder. Possibly lightning. Certainly electricity.

"Hi!"

Calm down. Right away. Except her heart didn't slow, and her hands wouldn't stay still. Fiddling with her dripping umbrella, she nearly poked herself in the eye with a loose metal spoke. *Buggeration.*

"Here, let me." Samuel grinned, then reached out and took her umbrella, neatly folded it and popped it into a container by the door. "Take a seat and I'll bring your order over."

She nodded, moving as if she was underwater and tethered to him. He pulled her closer with only a glance from under those velvety black eyelashes. But somehow, she found her table, setting herself up to write in her normal way.

Then, he was there with her order, standing opposite her seat. Instead of moving away as usual, he gestured at the empty chair opposite. She nodded, then sat perfectly still. The words inside her mind begged to come out.

Yes, please. Sit down, lie down, make yourself at home. Take off your shirt, if you like.

He spun the chair around and sat, legs astride, forearms leaning on the chair back. "I want to tell you something. Confide in you, I guess." He shrugged, the movement was tight, awkward. Almost nervous.

Why would he be nervous? She wanted to lean over and massage his shoulders.

"It's okay, you can tell me. I'm a good listener." She'd listen to anything he had to say from those lips, for hours. Even reciting the various coffee blends straight off the menu.

He nodded, and crinkled his forehead thoughtfully. "I had a difficult phone conversation last night with my girlfriend, Talia." His eyes flashed, dark pools with reflections of silver. She could drown in those eyes. "My *ex*-girlfriend, I should say. The thing is, she moved to London in January for work and it's been nine months. It's been hard, the long-distance thing. Anyway, she expected me to move over there at the end of the year and get married."

Her stomach dropped straight down to her steel capped combat boots, the cherry red ones today. He looked at her then and she met his gaze. Who knows what expression was on her face. Abject horror? Despair? *Getting married.* That was serious. Serious as murder. No, that wasn't fair. Some people liked being married. It probably had something to do with the people involved. The connection between them, the spark, mutual respect, understanding. Everything lacking in her marriage.

He cleared his throat. "You know they say 'absence makes the heart grow fonder', well, it didn't. Not for me. After a while I realised I was relieved Talia was gone. She was always pressuring me to get a proper job, to give up my music and working as a barista. Then the wedding. She started planning it two years ago, almost as soon as we got together. I felt like . . . a stand-in. A paper cut-out groom. She could've inserted any bloke into her plans. She didn't really want me. It wasn't like, true love."

Beth nodded, smiled, the kind of smile she used at work. It said, *Do go on, tell me more,* when really she meant, *Shut up, please.*

Her eyes popped open, triple-shot-espresso level wide awake. Wait, did he say it wasn't true love? He was the stand-in groom? She ought to be listening like she promised. Her mind whirred with too many thoughts, too many questions.

"So, are you going? To London?" She had to ask.

Please say no, please say no...

"No."

Yes! She tried to school her features. Not right to be so excited because he wasn't leaving or wasn't getting married. He was probably all broken inside. She shouldn't be hopeful.

"I called it off last night. We spoke for a long time, about everything. I told her I had a revelation. I don't want to leave Melbourne. My music's going great guns, I like this job and I've got a nice apartment. She's a top girl, but this is my home. She understood. I don't think she was surprised, after all." He sighed and ran his fingers through his hair. "And I told her there's this woman. Someone I'm interested in."

Her head instantly snapped up, her spine straight, at full attention. "Really? Someone you've known for a while?"

His expression softened, so warm and melty. "I've known her a while, but only in passing. I'd like to get to know her better. A lot better."

With that heart-stopping comment, he stood, pushed the chair back into the table. Walked away and disappeared behind the counter. A line of customers waited to place their orders. He must have left them waiting. To talk to her.

The remainder of her half-hour break blurred into a series of images in her mind. Samuel watching her under his lashes from behind the gleaming espresso machine. His smile when he opened the door for her that afternoon, when he'd been waiting for her. The curve of his firm denim-clad butt as he walked away from her table. She couldn't help that one slipping into her mind. The image was on frequent replay in her imagination.

When she left, the weather had changed for the better. The sun had popped out from behind the steel grey clouds, lighting up the city streets in golden reflections. There was even a faint rainbow, watery looking, but definitely there.

She made a wish and turned on her heel.

FRIDAY

A new day, a new start
Open up a man's heart
Give me a sign
And I'll make you mine

The upbeat song in her earbuds was perfect for her mood. She'd danced along the footpath, hardly noticing the darkening skies. Then she stopped in front of the blackboard, breathing in the poem like it was oxygen, vital to her survival. He'd put himself out there with those words, now he was asking her to do the same.

She hadn't mistaken his intentions yesterday, had she? *His intentions?* She'd been reading too much Jane Austen again.

Well, she wasn't a straight-laced Regency lady, sitting around drinking tea, waiting to be swept off her feet by a proper gentleman with a proposal. She was a little shy, it was true. But she wasn't a tea drinker. She liked coffee, and liked it strong, and when she knew what she wanted, she went for it. Just like with her writing, despite Pete and her boss and most of her friends telling her she was a fool for pursuing it.

She wanted Samuel. Wanted him like she wanted caffeine. But more so. She wanted to be with him like she wanted to write—with passion, with joy, for always, or as long as humanly possible. That was something.

Pushing open the door, she got inside without a hitch today. No stuck door. But also, no Samuel waiting for her. Pausing just inside, she scanned the long copper-panelled counter, the half-full tables by the windows, the leather-lined booths back near the kitchen. Hoping to find him hovering by one of the tables or walking through the swinging doors.

A young woman with blonde dreadlocks, wearing some sort of paisley kaftan, was on the register. She counted the money in the till, placing coins into plastic bags ready for banking. Beth wandered over to stand directly in front of Goldilocks.

She drummed her fingertips on the edge of the counter. "Hi, um, is Samuel around?"

"You must be Beth. Gorgeous woman with strawberry ringlets. He got that right." Goldilocks winked. *Okaaay.*

Wait a moment. Were those Samuel's words? He called her gorgeous? Little sparks of electric joy blew their fuses and warmed her whole body. Lighting her up.

Goldilocks tipped her head to one side, then grinned. "Sammy had to finish early but he'll be out in a sec. Take a seat. I'll bring your usual over."

Beth moved on auto-pilot, waiting to see what would happen next. For a creature of habit, this was all out of whack. Surreal. All Salvador Dali clocks melting over her landscape. Too much going on, too many bite-sized servings of crazy.

She plonked herself and her bag in their usual spots, retrieving her notebook and pen.

What could she say to him? Scribbling down notes, she plotted lines of dialogue more suited to a speech or a play. Too forced, too contrived. She crossed out what she'd written, trying to imagine the expression in his eyes when she asked him out. Prickles of anxiety poked at her insides, churning her stomach.

What if he said no? What if the woman he was interested in turned out to be someone else? She'd look like an utter nuff-nuff. She'd probably have to find a new café to haunt. It didn't bear thinking about.

Goldilocks appeared, coffee and chocolate truffle in hand. Without a word, she delivered the order, and left again with a wink. Beth devoured her truffle in only two bites. She needed the chocolatey goodness. Her coffee was fine, if a little plain. No love heart artwork today.

A few minutes later, she slowly packed up her things and glanced at the kitchen door. He wasn't going to show. Just when she'd worked up the nerve to ask him out, he'd left without even saying hello, or goodbye. She wandered to the front door, buttoned her coat and focused on the world outside through the window. Her heart sank with the view. Overcast. Showers. Raining on her parade. Of course.

Then, warmth wrapped around her with that distinctive spicy scent. His large hand on her shoulder warming her through layers of clothes. A jolt to her heart, his voice, smooth and so very male. "Beth. Wait."

He was here. Glancing over her shoulder, she took in the stunning view. He was close enough to see the tiny stubbly hairs on his jaw. His eyes sparkled with fascinating metallic glints.

She twisted her hands together and sucked in a breath. "I wanted to talk to you."

"I need to ask you something first."

"Okay." She nodded and turned towards him. What could he have to say?

"When I mentioned my ex, you didn't say you were married. Was that because you didn't want to upset me or because you still love him? Tell me the truth." He frowned and leaned on the door frame. "Your friend, Jenny, said you're not over your ex."

Her blood simmered like a coffee percolator in an American diner. That friend of hers was apparently a two-faced bitch.

"What? I'm divorced, divorced as can be. He ran off with our twenty-two year old neighbour. And since when are you talking to Jenny? Did she come back to see you?"

Was Jenny sniffing around Samuel? Her brain spun, hoping like hell Jenny hadn't touched him. Hadn't kissed him.

He raised his eyebrows. "Yeah, she dropped in." Huffing out a breath, he moved a step closer. "But that's not the point. I don't care about Jenny."

He touched Beth's upper arm, stroking his thumb up and down. She felt it everywhere, deep in hidden muscles that obviously needed attention. Samuel said he didn't want Jenny, but that didn't mean he was interested in her either. She pulled back, breaking the contact, folding her arms under her breasts.

Anger and tears struggled to win out. "That bloody bitch. She knew I liked you, but she still tried to steal you for herself." A groan rumbled in her chest. She had to get out. Now he'd know just how much she wanted him. She couldn't look at him.

She pushed her way through the door, straight into bucketing rain. Her light trench coat was no match for the downpour and her hair was instantly soaked. It stuck to her face in long wet strands, so she shoved it roughly back. Blinking her eyes shut to block out the rain, she opened them a second later to a great wall of manly chest. Wet, clinging t-shirt outlining muscles like a Greek god.

Samuel was right there, holding her umbrella. The one she'd forgotten yesterday. He popped it open and held it over their heads, protecting her from the great flood. Enveloping them in their own private bubble of warmth.

He lifted his free hand to her cheek, stroking the skin across her cheekbone. She shivered and sighed all at once.

His cocky grin made her lady parts clench. "So, you like me? I thought so, but I wanted to be sure. Sexually harassing the customers doesn't generally go down well with management."

A giggle escaped her lips. "But you wanted to harass me? Sexually?"

He groaned, the sweetest sound she'd ever heard. "Very much."

"The feeling is entirely mutual." She reached up and touched his chest as she'd wanted to so many times, pressing her hand flat against his pectoral muscle, right over his heart.

She smoothed his wet shirt down with her palm, once, twice, then ran her fingertip down the centre of his flat stomach. He sighed as if he'd never enjoyed anything so much. She sure hadn't. When she tipped her head up, his eyes had darkened a shade, if that was possible. Tiny silver raindrops glistened on the ends of his black lashes.

"Meet me tonight? My band's playing down the street at Thunder Bar."

He let go of her face and reached for something in his pocket. He passed her a card. An entry ticket, his phone number scrawled on the reverse. She gasped as his fingertips brushed hers. Molten chocolate fondant flowed through her belly, hot and sweet, a feeling so naughty it had to be a good sign.

"I'd love to." Her voice was breathier than ever, but she didn't care anymore. She wanted him to know how he affected her.

He leaned in, closer, still tentative, asking permission without words.

Yes, yes, yes!

Samuel's first kiss was feather-light, the barest brush of his lips against hers, but it seared her. Then he grasped her hip, pulling her close to his strong body. Reaching up, she ran her fingers along his jawline, the rough stubble rasping against her fingertips. He deepened the kiss and she opened to him, his tongue tangling with hers. His taste, combined with chocolate truffle and raindrops, so delicious, so decadent, she could have moaned aloud. Maybe she did.

She returned his kiss, pressing into him, wrapping her arms around his back. One of her hands found its way under his shirt and she gasped at the hot smoothness of his skin under her touch. She tasted his lips, the lower one so soft and full. Tilting her head to give him better access, she sighed when he broke contact with her mouth and kissed down her throat.

His hand found her bottom, pulling her tight into him. It was so good, she struggled to remember where they were. Outside. On a public street. The hard length of him pressed into her belly, unmistakable even through her trench and dress. Her inner muscles clenched, wanting him, now.

He groaned again and pulled back, kissing her softly on the mouth.

"See you tonight." He handed her the umbrella, checking she was okay to walk before letting go, stepping back a pace. "My Beth."

Her name on his lips held a promise of deliciousness to come.

Friday Night

Her breath
Her voice
Like an angel's wing
Taking me higher

Samuel's voice was transcendent, lifting high above the crowd. The slow ballad was a love song, pure and true. From her vantage point backstage in the wings, she watched every ripple of muscle along his arms and back, the way his body swayed as he sang. *Beautiful.*

Everything about him was beautiful. And he wanted her, as much as she wanted him. She hoped. The nervous fluttering in her belly was worse than butterflies now, like trapped pigeons in a cage, wings flapping madly and trying to escape.

It was nearly the end of the band's set. The guitarist was enjoying his solo, going off on a tangent. Samuel looked in her direction and grinned, bounding across the stage to her side as the song ended. He pulled her into his arms and kissed her full on the mouth, tasting her so thoroughly she nearly melted into the floor.

Then her fingers were in his hair, pulling him down into the kiss. His arms banded around her waist, holding her upright. Scattered kisses rained down on her cheekbones, nose and lips, before he stopped and stared into her eyes.

Whispering in her ear, he said, "I'm thinking we don't hang around for drinks. Give me two minutes."

She could only nod, beaming her approval of his excellent plan. Straightening her little black dress, a 60s crochet number with a plunging neckline, she hoped she looked the part. Rock chick girlfriend, not some old broad he'd picked up like an ancient groupie.

When his voice rang out again for one last song, she focussed. He was back in front of the band, really letting it rip. The music flowed through her body, washed over her mind. A soaring note ended the show, the stage lights fading to black, the crowd applauding. All of it second to him.

Beautiful. A beautiful present waiting to be unwrapped.

All hers. Maybe. She bit her lip.

"Beautiful, Beth." Samuel stood close behind her and slid her zip down her back, kissing the exposed nape of her neck and the sensitive spot between her shoulder blades.

Shivering, she tried not to second guess it. His lips, his touch, that's all there was. She closed her eyes, blocking out his unfamiliar, too trendy apartment. A bachelor pad. She was out of place.

Nerves made her tense up. Being close to him was like flying too close to the sun. Long forgotten sensations throbbed through her, her whole body demanding attention. Each part in turn. Her lips, her breasts, her stomach, her thighs, between her thighs. She wanted him inside her, like she'd never wanted any other man. But he was going so damn slow. And too fast.

Her dress dropped from her shoulders, down to her hips. *Too fast.*

What if he'd never seen a naked woman as old as her? What if she turned him off? Her eyes snapped open and she pulled her dress up to cover her breasts. She'd gone braless on account of the neckline, but without her dress she'd be truly naked, apart from a tiny scrap of black lace masquerading as underwear. Hardly battle armour. In case she needed to protect herself.

"Beth, what's wrong?" He urged her to turn in his arms.

She did, and instantly regretted it. He was so handsome. So overwhelming. She trembled, and he rubbed his hands up and down her arms, probably trying to soothe her. It turned her on and terrified her in equal measure.

"You're just so. . . handsome and strong and beautiful and talented and young, and your apartment is cool and hip and I'm just me. I'm old and kind of daggy and boring and only like one type of coffee. And Jenny said it's been so long since I've had sex I've probably dried up down there–"

There. He'd asked what was wrong, so she'd told him. She blushed down to her shoes. She'd probably have to

leave now, once she'd dug herself out of her pit of morti-
fication.

He didn't laugh, but his mouth curved up at the corners a
fraction. Fair enough. "Okay, so you're nervous. One thing at
a time. I like that you think I'm beautiful and strong and
talented. I'm flattered that you think so. Because I think all of
those same things about you. And you are not *old*. You're
gorgeous, from your hair to your stunning legs, and if I don't
see your breasts pretty soon I think I'm going to pass out.'

He grinned broadly, that cheeky dimple making an
appearance. "If you're boring, you're my type of boring. One
type of coffee? The type I make? It's the best. Of course you
like it." Stepping towards her, he twisted a lock of her hair
around his finger.

She hiccupped on a laugh, crossed with a small sob. He
was so lovely. "What about your apartment? It's too cool. I
feel like an imposter here." She gestured around wildly at
sculpted steel tables and lights that looked like spaceships.

She clutched her dress to her breasts as it slipped, only just
holding onto it. His eyes flicked down to her cleavage and
everything south of her belly button tightened.

"I'll let you in on a secret. I rented the apartment fully-
furnished from a mate who went gigging around Australia.
Most of it's not even my stuff. Except the photos. And the
bed."

Her laugh was a little more confident this time. Except
he'd mentioned his bed. Her heart pounded. Make or break,
this was it. He'd laid it all bare for her, more than once. Time
she did the same.

Her dress hit the floor with barely a whisper, but it was
like a thunderclap in the silent room. The only other sound
was Samuel's heavier-than-usual breathing. Matching
her own.

He stalked towards her, the final two steps. His gaze
roamed over her body as he spoke. "I think there was one

more objection we still need to clear up. Your so-called friend, Jenny. She said something quite rude and I think, totally untrue." Placing his large hand on her thigh, he shifted his hand up. Slowly, ever higher.

He'd almost reached the juncture of her thighs, the tiny scrap of lace barely covering her. Her skin was so hot, she might have singed her knickers.

Nearly incoherent with want, she'd forgotten what he was saying. "Hmmm?"

His hand cupped her swollen mound and she gasped when his fingertips skirted the hem of her underwear. Everything throbbed and tingled when he worked her tender flesh, back and forth, finding her centre. Her breathing was shallow, her hips moving to meet his touch.

"She was wrong. Nothing's dried-up at all. You're so wet, Beth."

"Oh, God. Samuel!" She cried out as her pleasure peaked, strong and unexpected. And perfect. So, so perfect. Pulses of light flashed behind her closed eyelids as she rocked into his touch.

When she stilled, he pulled his hand away but then wrapped her in his arms so tightly she almost burst. He kissed her lips, like before at the gig, deep and passionate. A bud of something ridiculous, something like love, blossomed inside her. She should've stamped on it, killed it before it took root. And yet, she wanted that little flower to bloom.

"Now that you're properly relaxed," he said, grinning, "I think it's time I take you to bed, young lady." He smacked her on the butt with his palm, not hard, but she yelped.

"Oh, fuck yes." The words popped out before she could second guess herself.

His eyes widened and heat lit his gaze with a wicked glint. And then she laughed so hard, he actually had to pick her up and carry her.

Straight to bed.

SATURDAY MORNING

My Beth
Naked
Pretty as a rose petal
In my bed
Stay. Forever, or as long as you'll have me.

Beth pulled the crisp sheets up to her chin. God, he was sweet. Sweet and delicious and passionate and tender. She grinned as she read the handwritten note again, before smoothing out the creases and laying it flat on the empty pillow beside her.

Samuel must be up – she heard noises somewhere nearby. Probably the kitchen. Her stomach grumbled. She'd had quite a workout, nearly all night long.

She must have closed her eyes again but opened them when the wafting scent of fresh coffee hit her square in the pleasure centre of her brain. She was already salivating before Samuel walked through the bedroom door. He was only wearing a brief pair of black boxers. She licked her lips to keep from dribbling. Sitting half upright in bed, she held the sheet up to cover herself.

"Don't cover up on my account. I like you naked. All pink and pretty." His naughty smile made her drop the sheet. Modesty be damned.

He'd stalked to her side of the bed and put down the breakfast tray he'd been carrying. The delicious aromas wafted her way before she spied toast, eggs and bacon, beautiful-looking coffee adorned with roses and love hearts on top. And chocolate truffles. Lots of them, in a glass dish.

Samuel leaned over her, resting one knee on the edge of the bed. "I'll taste these little pink treats again now." He pressed his lips to her left nipple, rasping his tongue across the peak.

Hot sensation shot straight to her core, making her gasp. Then he turned his attentions to her other breast. Panting already, she threaded her fingers through his hair, but then he pulled his head away.

She glanced at the tray on the bedside table. "Aren't we going to eat this gourmet breakfast?"

"Mmmm, in a minute. Maybe twenty." He'd moved up her body, half sitting, half leaning over her. He bit her lower lip. She licked across it and he groaned, low and long.

God, that sound. I love it.

Running her fingers down his spine, she whispered, "How about a deal? We have dessert first, breakfast later."

"My kind of woman."

He lifted the glass dish from the tray and she noticed something shiny underneath. A foil packet glittered in the pale sunlight streaming through his apartment window.

She laughed, lifted the condom packet and waved it in front of his face.

"I meant the chocolate truffles for dessert, not more sex. Not that there's anything wrong with sex."

"Damn right there's nothing wrong. Everything is in full working order." He pressed his body fully against hers and she realised he was absolutely right.

Full working order. Ready to go. *How fantastic.*

"How about I help you out with this," she said, waving the condom packet again, "and you help me eat the truffles."

"Absolutely. Great minds think alike and all that." He rolled to one side and got rid of his boxers, letting her take the lead.

She tore open the foil and rolled the condom down his erection in one smooth movement. If her hands were shaking, he didn't seem to notice.

She worked her hand up and down, until he groaned so loud he probably woke the whole building. She didn't mind. Hell, she'd wrap herself in that sound forever if she could. He pressed himself down over her body and her thighs just parted for him. Wrapping her legs around his waist, she clung to his shoulders. Then he nudged her entrance and plunged straight inside her.

She cried out, loving the feel of him so deep, his head on her shoulder, kissing her there.

"Good?" he asked, beginning to move.

"So good."

"You know, I meant it. The poem."

It took her a second to realise what he was talking about, as he thrust deep. Today's poem, the note on the pillow. The way he was pressing that perfect spot inside her, making her body sing, it was kind of distracting. In the best possible way.

He nibbled her earlobe, making her shudder. "Stay with me. Forever, or as long as you'll have me."

Her heart bubbled over with happiness. This sexy man, so sweet. For whatever reason, he wanted her. Then he swivelled his hips, grinding down on her, and she nearly came undone. She'd never known any pleasure like it. He already knew her body so well. He seemed to know her, yet they'd only been together a few short hours.

She didn't want to over-think this. Playing it safe hadn't worked out in the past. Jumping head first into adventure and pleasure might be the way to go from now on.

"Yes." That breathy voice of hers was back. Probably for good.

"Yes, you're going to come, or yes, you'll stay with me?" He bore down on her again, sending small shards of sparkling joy zipping through her core.

"Both! Yes!"

Everything tightened, focused on the place where they were joined. Her climax rolled through her in hot waves, so intense it stole her words. Tears prickled behind her eyes, but he was there, kissing her, deep and slow, still rocking into her, making her gasp her pleasure again and again. She loved it. She loved him.

Then his movements became more ragged, more uncontrolled and she loved that too. The way he was lost in the moment with her.

When he cried out, she thought her heart would explode. Just one word, her name. The most beautiful sound she'd heard from his lips. He collapsed on top of her, nuzzling into her neck.

She stroked her hands down his back, enjoying the strong musculature and smoothness. All that manliness. All hers.

After a couple of minutes of quiet, listening to the sound of his steady breathing, inhaling his spicy male scent, she had to say something. "Thanks, Samuel."

"For what?"

"For being patient with me last night."

He rose up above her, supporting himself on his arms. "You're thanking me? Thank you for going out with me. For giving me a shot. For staying in with me too."

Grinning at each other like the crazy fools they probably were, she realised one thing. They still had an awful lot of truffles to get through.

She bit her lip, a naughty idea forming. "So, about the truffles. Are they kind of a package deal with you?"

"Mmmm. Absolutely." He kissed her throat.

"You sure know how to treat a girl."

He rolled off her with the cheekiest smile she'd seen. She sucked in a breath, needing a moment to collect herself.

"Back in a sec." He got up and strolled off through the adjoining door. She whistled her approval at the fine rear view. His answering chuckle echoed from the bathroom.

She shifted into action so when he returned, she'd be ready. One truffle between her teeth and the glass dish holding the rest sitting on the bed beside her. She pushed back the sheets so she lay naked, ready to tempt him.

He opened the door – she heard the snick of the lock – and then nothing. Dead silence. Then he dropped whatever he'd been holding with a thud and rushed to the side of the bed. He kissed her mouth, biting the truffle in half. Devouring it, and her. Everything in her whole body tingled and sighed, kissing him, tasting the sugary smoothness, the cocoa butteriness, the whole kit and caboodle. Tasting those full lips and the truffle in one astonishing morsel. But she was ready for more.

Samuel lay beside her, his naked torso aligning with her side. He picked up another truffle from the dish and held it up near her mouth and licked his lips. "You're a genius, Beth. I think I love you."

Her heart thudded, those pesky tears prickling again. Joy rising up, she laughed with a lightness she hadn't felt in years.

She breathed out, then dived in. Headlong. Brave. "You know, it's funny you should say that. I think I love you too."

Before she could say another word, he'd placed another truffle on his tongue and captured her lips in a delicious, never-ending kiss.

Tree Love

A Romantic Short Story

Cassandra O'Leary

Natalia Bianchi wasn't shy about getting what she wanted. Until she met The Man. Dan 'The Man' Mancini was everything she wanted, in a beautiful, six-foot-three package of yum, begging to be unwrapped. But she didn't. Unwrap him.

Natalia sat quietly beside him, her nose in a book, as usual. Learning about the history of garden design wasn't usually so stimulating. She kept notes in her leather-bound sketchbook, decorating the margins with drawings from life and memory. Leaves, flowers. A vitally strong man's hands...

Natalia and Dan were study buddies. That was all. Study sessions in the university Arts library's private study rooms were painful. In a low down, throbbing, sweet and sinful way. It wouldn't have been so bad, so arousing, except it had been going on for a year. She squeezed her thighs together under the table.

Straightening her spine, she gathered her courage. Now or never. *Now.*

Thumping her book closed, she glanced at Dan. He watched her, tilting his head to the side, his full lips slightly parted. Dark, wavy hair flopped over one ebony eye, sparkling with awareness. His scent was the forest in spring, both earthy and herbally-fresh.

Natalia approached him in two strides and climbed onto his lap before she changed her mind.

His eyes were wide, but he didn't move. "What's up, Nat?" he asked, his gaze dropping to her mouth.

She wrapped her arms around his neck, inhaling so his scent filled her nostrils. Dan's groan rumbled through her body like earth tremors, and molten lava flowed between them.

She leaned in and pressed her lips to his. Tasting him,

teasing him, she nipped at his lips with tiny kisses. Then he bit her bottom lip, giving it a gentle tug. She flung herself at him, pressing into his chest, hot through his clinging t-shirt.

Opening her lips under his, she tasted him—an explosion of bittersweet chocolate and the headiest hit of that herbal scent. Tongues clashed and slid together until she was gasping. Slanting her head for a better angle, she licked across his delicious lower lip and kissed him deeper.

His large hand had moved to her hip, grasping her close to his body. His hardening body.

She made the kind of noise usually reserved for devouring chocolate covered almonds. *Study buddies?* All bets were off.

He broke the kiss. "Natalia." His voice came out choked. Resting his forehead against hers, his chest rose and fell in a ragged rhythm.

Dan kissed her forehead, then lifted her to standing as if she weighed nothing. He grabbed his notebook and swaggered out of the room without saying another word.

She'd shocked him into silence.

Natalia slid down on her chair, still panting, letting her head flop onto her sketchbook. It would be okay. They'd talk about the kiss tomorrow.

***

PRESENT DAY

Emails pinged her inbox in furious succession. Natalia shook her head. *Work, work, work.* So many trees, so little time.

The city council's latest scheme was keeping her busy as admin officer. Driving her bonkers. Assigning email addresses to trees. *Hmmm.* Some bright spark in Marketing and Public Affairs decided to take direct reports from citizens about vandalism or sick trees, all for PR.

Exhibit A: an email about vandals cutting bark off street trees with knives. Short, factual. She nodded, clicking at her keyboard, forwarding it to the work team. The horticultural staff may still save those trees.

Natalia scrolled through the messages, prioritising as she went. Potential issues were marked with red flags or known troublemakers with exclamation marks. For someone else to deal with 'up the chain'. Thank goodness.

Who knew Melbourne's city dwellers would be so interested in the trees in the parks and gardens? Not her, and she was mad about plants. She had no idea what to do with the unusual emails, letters and...poems.

To: OakTree21@melbparks.com
From: caro@sparkynet.com
Subject: My heart

Dear Oak Tree 21,
    My heart worships the mighty oak tree,
    Spreading love and shading the ground,
    With your leaves,
    Like flakes of green happiness.
    Thank you, Mighty Oak Tree!
    I'd kiss you but I may chap my lips.
    Yours, Caroline.

Okay, then. Caroline obviously had some issues but contacting the Tree-mail hotline probably wouldn't help. Natalia hit the pre-written response for the crazies.

Thank you for your feedback. The Parks and Gardens department appreciates your interest in our trees.

Natalia wasn't sure she did appreciate their interest. But work was work. She swivelled in her chair and leaned over her notepad. A half-finished sketch of oak leaves and acorns drew her gaze. She grabbed her pencil in a sure grip, shading around a barely-defined leaf. Then her phone buzzed. A reminder to herself to pay her electricity bill. This month's budget would be a stretch.

Dropping her pencil, she sighed, breath leaking from her lungs like air from a deflated balloon. A masters degree in art history and botanical drawing, in particular, prepared her fantastically well for a career in damn close to jack shit.

She reached for her Japanese ceramic cup. The fresh jasmine scent cleansed her mind, but the green tea burned her palate. *Too hot!* A strangled yelp escaped her lips. With a splutter, she wiped the drips from her chin with a tissue.

"Hey, Babe, you all right?" The voice from behind the green partition printed with eucalyptus leaves, made her jump on her swivel chair.

Natalia put down her cup with a clunk before she scalded herself properly. "I'm fine."

Her friend's head popped up over the partition. "You coming for a walk at lunchtime?" Sofia was her bestie and trendy girl around town. Her black and gold streaked hair dangled from behind her ears.

"Sure, Sof. Botanical Gardens okay with you?"

"You bet. And afterwards, there's a fab new Spanish tapas place nearby. You've got to try their gambas a la plancha."

Natalia patted her belly, which rumbled on cue. Sofia knew the best lunch spots. "Sounds awesome, but what the hell is a gum-bus?"

"Gambas. Grilled prawns with chilli dipping sauce so delicious it nearly made me O." Sofia fanned herself with one hand.

Natalia giggle-snorted. Sounded like a meal worth blowing the budget on. "Sold. Let's go."

Natalia's pale curls blew around wildly, sticking to her lip gloss in the fresh breeze. It was bracing for February. Goosebumps pebbled her bare arms. She trudged the gravel path beside Sofia, across the sloping lawns of the gardens.

Sofia slowed and nudged Natalia's arm. "Babe, isn't that your oak tree?"

Natalia glanced in the direction her friend pointed. "It's not my bloody oak tree. It's just popular," she mumbled.

Some students were sprawled on beach towels under the enormous tree, near the herbaceous border. One chick had her shirt off, stripped down to her bra. It wasn't hot weather, but she obviously thought she was smokin'.

Natalia sighed. A few years ago, that would have been her, going to class and then hanging with friends in the park. She wouldn't have got her boobs out though. Unless someone like Dan 'The Man' Mancini had asked nicely. Then she might've done enough to get arrested. Sadly, she'd never needed bail money.

Sofia stopped mid-stride, her ankle boots scraping the gravel. She pointed, silently raising her eyebrows and licking her fire-engine-red painted lips.

Natalia's gaze followed her friend's fingertip to a man sporting the most impressive forearms and muscular shoulders she'd ever seen. Her eyes roved lower, down the ladder he stood on, leaning against the infamous oak tree.

The man wore khaki overalls with a tight black t-shirt underneath. Workman's gear. Showing off bare biceps, flexing and bunching under suntanned skin. It shouldn't have turned her on, but boy, it did good things. Low down, clenchy things.

His butt was pure perfection. Globes of rounded,

muscular man-flesh, begging to be squeezed through the canvas fabric. She could have sworn they called her name.

"Natalia?" He'd turned on his perch to stare straight at her. Dark, brooding eyes lit with humour, under a mop of wavy black hair. Sparks of recognition zipped through her brain.

Bugger me.

Dan The Man, in the flesh.

Dan Mancini looked fine as ever–even larger than she remembered. And he was in her garden. Under her oak tree. Clipping her foliage. Trimming her undergrowth. The spot between her thighs pulsed. Her lady garden needed some attention, forget the trees.

Natalia cleared her throat and stepped forward. "Dan Mancini. Well, I never."

No, she never had. For years, she'd regretted the lack of touching him. Ever since he'd abruptly left university after one searing kiss.

Stepping down the ladder's rungs, he jumped and thudded to ground. He wiped his brow against one bronzed forearm. He was all dirty and sweaty. In a good way. Dan strolled towards her, his hips swinging in that loping style she remembered. Like a cowboy.

He smiled, and her heart tried to jump out of her throat. "You're a sight for sore eyes. Nat, you look sensational."

His close inspection of her fitted black dress, bare legs, down to her strappy red sandals, made heat rise from her throat to her cheeks. Her face would be as scarlet as her shoes. At least she'd be colour coordinated.

Sofia giggled and nudged Natalia in the ribs. "I'll get going. Leave you two to catch up." She wandered off down the garden path.

Natalia's lips popped open to tell her friend to stay, but her heart wasn't in it. The *thump, thump, thump* beneath her breasts beat only for Dan. She didn't want to share. Even if her old study buddy was a stranger these days. A simmer of long-ago anger rose to the boil. Why hadn't he stayed in touch?

"What were you doing in my tree?" Natalia crossed her arms and stared at him.

Dan's lips quirked upwards. He looked edible when he smiled. "*Your* tree? I think this tree belongs to all the taxpayers of Melbourne, myself included."

Her heart picked up speed. Did he say he moved to Melbourne? "I work for Parks and Gardens, so it is one of my trees. You live here now?"

He nodded. "Going on six months. It's great to be back."

Dan skipped town for Sydney ten years ago. He shouldn't be here. Not now, when it was too late. Natalia tucked her left hand under her armpit. The diamond on her ring finger cut into her flesh. She wasn't trying to hide it exactly, but she wasn't showing it off either.

It was about six months since she'd accidently started dating her boss, Ted. Coffee turned into drinks after work, one date led to another. Before she'd made a conscious decision, they were 'a thing'. A few months later, he'd proposed. Not in an overly romantic way. He'd sent an email. Suggested they save a date in the calendar. Ted said they should make it official. So, they were engaged and had slept together two, forgettable, times.

Ted was a nice guy, a bit older, but stable. He put up with her flaky, disorganised self. More than she could say for most guys she'd dated. They didn't get her. Nobody ever had, except Dan.

Once upon a time, she'd dreamed of more. A partner, a lover, who made her laugh and sigh with pleasure. Someone strong and dependable who'd never leave. But waiting around for a prince got old quickly, and modern princesses had to work to buy their own castles.

Ted was a kind, quiet man who wouldn't annoy her if they shared a house. Surely, she'd made the right decision.

Ted didn't really appreciate her drawings though. What would he think if he actually visited her studio apartment, full to the exposed metal rafters with sketches and water-colours, easels and paintbrushes, specimens of flowers and bark? Her own, private artist's jungle.

Dan dipped his chin at the small folio tucked under her arm. "Are you still drawing? I always loved your sketches. Especially the fern frond. I still have it on my wall. You saw beauty in the smallest details."

Swoon! Her knees wobbled. How could he say something so sweet? Her future husband hadn't.

Was it possible Dan remembered everything? They'd spent hours together in the university library and in parks like this, and she'd been constantly sketching. Maybe he remembered their one and only kiss. She'd replayed it count-less times, only with a different ending. A dirty, sweaty, happy ending.

Her insides fluttered like an autumn leaf falling from a branch. She shouldn't be thinking about him this way. She shook her head. "I have to go. See you round, maybe."

Dan's black eyebrows cinched together. "Okay. See you."

She hurried off down the path towards the city.

"Hey, Nat!" He called and she couldn't help turning back. "I'm working on site here for a couple of months, if you want to grab a coffee one day."

She sighed. Of course she wanted to. But she shouldn't. Still, she didn't say no. "Put me down as a definite maybe."

His answering grin was seared on her brain as she fled. Back to work, and her fiancé.

The next day, Natalia sketched a banksia flower at her desk, when the familiar ping of an email sent her scuttling to her keyboard.

To: admin@melbparks.com

From: dmancini@alberoamore.com.au

Subject: Sketches for research project

To the Parks and Gardens team,

I'm a tree surgeon/horticulturalist working in the Botanic Gardens for the next two months. I'm recording the change of seasons for a research project in partnership with the Melbourne Museum. Could you please put me in touch with a recommended botanical artist?

Regards,

Dan Mancini.

The email swam before her eyes. Warmth bloomed in her belly like a rose opening its petals. Dan had emailed her. Well, he'd emailed the department, looking for a botanical artist, probably an attempt to find her.

His email address was interesting: dmancini@alberoamore.com.au. *Albero amore.* Her late grandmother had taught her basic Italian. She recognised the words for 'tree' and 'love'. Dan worked for a company called Tree Love? That was perfect. He'd become a horticulturalist. One with brawn and brains, by the sound of the research project. Beneath the handsome exterior was a mind to be reckoned with, as she'd always known.

Natalia fiddled with her engagement ring as she re-read the email. The ring was too loose – it had never fit right. She'd been meaning to get it re-sized.

"Natalia, can I have a word? It's about dinner on Friday." Ted had snuck up behind her, stealthy as fog on a misty Melbourne morning.

Her body went stiff as Ted stroked her shoulder.

Glancing behind her, she caught Ted reading her email on

her PC. She hated that. "What about it? I've booked the restaurant for seven o'clock."

Ted frowned, his hazel eyes sliding sideways. Paying no attention to what she was saying, only thinking about what he'd say next. "I don't think it's the right setting. Too noisy and crowded. I'd prefer somewhere elegant."

Right. Most people said she had great taste. She wasn't as trendy as Sofia, but she knew good food, especially Italian. The bistro she'd chosen was the best on Lygon Street, Melbourne's 'Little Italy'.

"If you have another suggestion, I can check if they have a free table."

Unlikely for a group of six, but she was trying. Trying to get along with Ted's friends, years older than herself. And his ex-wife. The ever-present Bettina, who didn't behave like an ex-anything. *She* was trying.

He leaned over, reading her screen again. "Will do. What's this email about?"

Natalia folded her arms. Should she tell Ted that she knew Dan? She shrugged. "He's a horticulturalist, looking for a botanical artist for a special project." She left it at that, carefully shading around the outlines of her sketchy statement.

"You should meet him. That's your sort of thing, right?" His voice was chirpy. Pleased with himself for remembering her 'hobby'. Her art.

She closed her eyes. Decision made. "Yes. It's exactly my sort of thing."

Natalia couldn't see Dan as she hurried past the lake, onto the green lawn surrounded by specimen trees. She'd arranged to meet him at ten o'clock but was running late. She power-walked, but still took in the shimmering sunshine reflecting off the water, ducks swimming, and the city skyline poking through the tree-tops in the distance.

Scanning the surrounding landscape, she spotted him up a tree, or rather hanging off a pencil-straight Norfolk Island Pine. The system of ropes and pulleys looked complicated. She strolled to the base of the pine and waited, craning her neck. Up, almost to the sky.

Dan wore stereotypical lumberjack gear. Well-loved Levi's and a red checked flannel shirt. Nothing wrong with that. *Nope.* An urban lumberjack. Exactly Dan's style. Hers too, if she had to pick a fantasy-boyfriend look.

A safety helmet covered his head, but the rear view was outstanding as he descended. Completely in control, Dan lowered himself, rappelling off the tree trunk, making it look easy.

He hollered on the way down to earth. "Nat, helllooo!"

Landing with a thud, he grinned as he pulled off the helmet and unhooked the abseiling harness around his hips.

She laughed, surprising herself. She'd skipped breakfast due to nerves. "Good to see you again."

Damn, what an understatement. Her eyes drank him in like a fine Italian wine, when she'd been subsisting on piss-weak light beer. From his delicious grin and stubble coated jaw to his flashing ebony eyes, his face was perfection. It would take her years to describe him in words. Pencils or paints were her language. She'd love to sketch him again.

Her one sketch of him at university was still a prized possession. He was hidden away with a bunch of pressed flowers and concert tickets, in the folio usually stashed under her bed. It was now out on her desk.

Dan gestured to a picnic blanket and knapsack near a park bench. "Come sit down."

He sat, stretching his long legs out in front of him. The man took up space. She remembered, from sitting close together in a library study room. The air was always thick in that confined space. Out in the open, her skin still tingled with awareness, and his earthy scent teased her senses, making her giddy.

Natalia lowered herself onto the blanket. In denim shorts and a white t-shirt, her skin seemed over-exposed. And hot.

Dan glanced at her, then leaned forward looking out over the lawn. "Thanks again for coming. I'm rapt you agreed to help with the project." His voice was low and husky, almost conspiratorial. As if they shared a secret. Maybe they did.

She hoped the project wasn't the only reason he'd contacted her.

Watching him, she leaned back and rested her weight on her palms. "Are you really looking for a botanical artist? Or have you lured me onto your picnic blanket under false pretences?"

Dan's smile was naughty. He rubbed his stubbled jaw. "Both. I want an artist, and I really want you."

Thud. Her heart slammed against her rib cage.

Dan's eyes poured over her, slick as paint poured on canvas. When she risked a glance at him, he wasn't checking out her legs or her boobs in her tight shirt. He was staring at her hand.

Her left hand. The Ring.

"I can explain…" Could she? How could she explain a relationship, an engagement, that she didn't understand herself?

Ted hadn't mentioned love, but neither had she. The closest she'd come to feeling that emotion had been with the man sitting beside her.

Years ago, she'd thought she and Dan had something special. From her perspective, their one-and-only kiss had meant everything. But any artist knew, perspective was a trick of the eye and the mind. It depended on where you stood. Dan had left Melbourne the very next day. Without saying goodbye.

She gulped in fresh air, trying not to let the old hurt cut again. She had more on her mind. The arrangement with Ted wasn't working. Her instant attraction to Dan only underlined the fine print, all she was missing out on. But extricating herself from the engagement could be tricky.

"It's okay. You don't have to explain to me." Dan lay down with his hands behind his head. "I should be the one explaining."

She glanced at him and her heart shuddered. Dan in serious mode wore the hard-jawed expression of a man carved from a mountain. Like a dead President on Mount Rushmore. But more handsome.

"I didn't want to leave Melbourne when we were at uni. But I was only nineteen and Dad needed me. He couldn't keep the gardening business going. It was his heart. He passed away two years later. I kept the business running and made it a success. It's what he wanted."

Natalia reached out and stroked her fingertips along his jaw. A needy sound rose from his throat, a sigh crossed with a groan. She pulled back, as if burned.

Touching him was a mistake, unless she gave up everything. Forgot about Ted. Unless she was brave enough to reach for Dan, with all she had.

She turned and whipped open her sketch book with trembling fingers, fumbling for a pencil in her bag. She needed to do something with her hands. She wanted to capture his expression. And it was easier to talk when she drawing.

As she sketched, the words flowed. "Ted and me. We're engaged, but it's no fairytale. It's an arrangement that suits us both. At least, it did. We're friends." She sketched Dan's face – the broad sweep of his eyebrows, sharp planes of his cheekbones. And that jaw. "Not best friends though. I'm having second thoughts."

She hadn't said that out loud before.

Huffing out a shaky breath, she kept her eyes on her drawing. A lock of Dan's hair falling across his forehead. On the page, it framed his eyes to perfection.

Dan shifted, leaning forward. "You deserve more. A man who'll love you, adore you, until the end of the world." He brushed his hand across her fingers, until it rested on top of hers. She tensed, almost pulled away. But he encircled her wrist with his enormous hand, making a bracelet, stroking his thumb back and forth across her pulse point.

Heat rushed through her body and her heart skittered. She dropped her sketchbook and pencil with a clatter and wisp of pages fluttering.

He spoke, and even the wind quieted. "Once upon a time, there was a fairytale kingdom. A young knight visited every day for a year, in a castle filled with books instead of treasure. There was a beautiful princess, with golden curls and amazing eyes. Sometimes green, sometimes blue. Like the sea, or the sky through the treetops."

Releasing her hand, he fell back on the blanket, gazing through the leafy canopy. "The knight didn't belong there. Not in the castle, inside with the books. He was a peasant who belonged outside, in the fields. The princess was the only reason to stay. The kingdom was barred to people like him without a fortune. He'd climbed the gates with sheer determination, but he had to leave."

Slowly, she lowered herself until she lay on her side. Watching. Listening. The shadowplay across his face was hypnotic. Leaves shimmered in greyscale, mottling his olive skin. Dan was in his element.

Dan's voice dropped lower, so she shuffled closer. His body heat enveloped her like a cocoon. "I was never good enough for you, not smart or rich enough. But I never forgot the brilliant artist I fell for. One day the knight came home, older and wiser. He hoped the princess would remember him too."

"She remembers everything." Her gaze fixed on his lips.

He sighed, as his gaze flickered over her face, from her eyes to her mouth. "But the princess was engaged to be married."

Natalia propped herself up on her elbow. "This is why I hate fairytales. All that woe and drama, when a proper conversation could have solved everything. Dan, I always thought you were smart. And who cares about rich? I wanted you then. I want you now. If you'd asked me when I was nineteen, I would have gone to Sydney with you in a heart-beat." Her heart beat quicker now, out of control, blood pounded in her ears.

She wanted him, even now. She'd said it.

Dan stared down at her. His dark eyes glittered below a creased forehead. "I didn't think you were interested. When you kissed me, I understood you were saying goodbye. Everyone knew I was leaving. The gossip was crazy, but I wasn't going to jail or sailing solo around the world."

Natalia blinked a few times so her eyeballs didn't pop out of her head. "Saying goodbye? Oh, Dan. I didn't hear any gossip. I had my head down, studying and finishing some artworks. Next thing I knew, you'd already left. I finally heard you'd gone to live with your Dad in Sydney."

She reached for him. Somehow, her fingers threaded through the curls at the nape of his neck. "I couldn't under-stand why you didn't call or email. I missed you so much, but I thought you didn't care."

He touched her face, his large hand rough and warm against her cheek. "Natalia."

Her heart pinched. He never called her Natalia, always Nat. Except one time, after their first kiss.

Dan's warm breath brushed her cheek. "I regretted the

way I left. You have to know, I cared about you. So damned much. All these years later, I had to find you. Tell me it's not too late for us."

She sighed. "It's not too late."

He leaned in, stroking his thumb over her cheekbone.

Natalia sucked in a breath. His lips touched hers, setting her whole body trembling. She tasted him again, so delicious, so familiar, like coming home.

He urged her lips to part, sliding his tongue against hers in a sensual dance, kissing her deeply. So deeply she felt it in her toes. Her heart. She wanted him, all of him.

But she had to do this right.

She pulled back, resting her head on his shoulder. "Just give me one day."

Dan nodded, wrapping her in his arms.

Natalia stood outside Ted's office at lunchtime and gave a small, embarrassed knock.

It was now or never. *Now.*

She stepped inside and shut the door behind her with a click.

Ted looked up and smiled, friendly as always. He was her friend. But nothing else. There was no thudding beat from her heart, no melting expression in his eyes. No promises that couldn't be broken.

"We need to talk, about us." A lame opening line. But true. "I need to call off the engagement." Straight to the point. Ted would appreciate that.

His expression was a picture. Not sadness or anger though. Bewilderment? His greying eyebrows were raised.

"Just like that? I know I haven't spent enough time with you lately. I'm sorry."

He stood, staying behind his desk. The space between them seemed vast.

She stepped towards him. "I'm sorry, Ted. It's just not what I want anymore."

He let out a shaky breath. "Okay. But tell me honestly, did I do something wrong? Bettina said I was so wrapped up in work, I didn't pay her any attention."

Natalia nodded. "Bettina's right. A woman needs to feel special. Not like an extra box to tick on your to-do list."

Ted frowned, staring at his handcrafted timber desk, covered in reams of paperwork.

Natalia's stomach twisted in knots. Hadn't she thought the same? Marriage was something she should get onto. She was nearly thirty, so she'd tick it off her list, like doing the washing.

She looked down at her clenched hands. A glint of light caught her eye. Sunlight streamed through the slatted blinds on the window, bounced off her hand and split into rainbow colour. *The ring.* She slid the gold band off, then held it out on her flat palm.

Ted stepped past his desk to the centre of the room. Met her in the middle. He took the ring but watched it closely, as if it might explode. "What am I supposed to do with this?"

Natalia's lips stretched into a wry smile. "Give it to Bettina. I think she'd say yes. Again. If you paid attention, you might have noticed she never really left."

Ted's face brightened instantly.

She knew he was still in love with his ex-wife. Her stomach-knots untwined. "Goodbye, Ted." She turned to leave, but paused with her hand on the doorknob. "Well, not goodbye. I still work here, unless that's too weird."

"It's not weird. See you at the meeting later." He stuffed

the ring into his jacket pocket. "Give us an update on the project with the horticulturalist. It sounds promising."

She grinned. "Thanks Ted. It will be amazing."

One year and one day later

Natalia wiped her damp palm down her ivory silk sheath dress. Her hands shook as she held up the printed email.

She glanced up and met Dan's smiling eyes. The backdrop of the gardens and the oak tree was magnificent, but not as beautiful as this man in a suit. He was divine.

Natalia cleared her throat and read the words she'd written in advance.

To: oaktree21@melbparks.com
From: natalia@melbparks.com
CC: dmancini@alberoamore.com.au
Subject: Tree love
Dear Oak Tree 21,
I'm no good with words.
I sometimes get tongue-tied
Or forget to speak till it's nearly too late.
I'm more eloquent with pencil or brush,
But meeting my love under your branches was fate.
Meeting him again, not just for a day.
This time, forever.
Thank you, beautiful oak tree.
Yours always,
Madly in tree love,
Mrs Natalia Mancini.
"Kiss the man," Sofia urged from her side.
Bossy bridesmaid.

Natalia reached for Dan's lapel. "I will."

Dan's smile was devastating. "I love you."

He was hers. When their lips met, she sighed with the kind of happiness she'd read about in fairytales.

The forever kind.

Girl Under The Christmas Tree

A Steamy Holiday Romance Novella
(Girl On A Plane Series 0.5)

Cassandra O'Leary

Author's Note

ON GIRL UNDER THE CHRISTMAS TREE

Dear reader,

This story is a prequel of sorts or 'origin story' and companion piece to my debut novel, *Girl on a Plane*, published by HarperCollins UK in 2016. I loved re-visiting the minor character of Yuki, back before she became a flight attendant with Mermaid Airlines. I've given her a fun backstory with plenty of romance. *Girl Under The Christmas Tree* has a happy for now (HFN) ending, leaving Yuki's future wide open. I may have to write another spin off story like this!

Happy reading,

Cassandra x

Chapter One

The Palladian Hotel, Melbourne, Australia
A few years ago...

Yuki wasn't the type of girl to say no to opportunity when it came knocking, or even when it came swaggering into the five-star hotel reception area dressed in a crumpled three-piece suit. God, how she was a sucker for a man in a tailored three-piece suit.

She'd nabbed the best spot in the foyer, a cushy seat under the hotel's ginormous Christmas tree, which was covered in sparkly lights and glass ornaments. She was busy staring into space, about to scoff a Christmas cookie and a café latte in a reusable cup, when she spotted him coming her way. Since she was on a break, she wasn't quite prepared to be questioned by the man.

He cleared his throat, and she glanced at him, then did an actual, cartoon style, double take when she saw his face. *Handsome stranger alert...*

"Excuse me, but I was wondering if you could point me in the direction of the Grand Ballroom. I found a big room over there," he gestured over his shoulder, "but it isn't particularly grand."

Oh. My. God. He was Irish. The devastating charm Irish men had in spades, was her personal Kryptonite. Everyone knew it. The way he said the word *grand* made her want to bite her tongue before she accidentally swallowed it. And there was more.

She let her gaze travel all the way up the full height of him, to take in the kind of perfect face that made her wish she could draw portraits. His eyes were incredibly blue and sparkly, and contrasted with his wavy hair, a kind of mahogany, almost black with a hint of warm red.

Assessment: very attractive. Strong jaw, a little dark stubble, nice large hands. He held a leather briefcase in front of him, and she was staring at his hands like a weirdo hand stalker.

He smiled and she almost cried. His teeth were perfect, like movie star teeth. Did real people have smiles that lit up a room like a string of high wattage Christmas tree lights? Apparently, yes.

If she had been standing behind the reception desk she would have been more polished, more professional. Probably less pouty. She'd only wanted to have her cookie and eat it too! Was that too much to ask? Apparently. But she wanted to talk to him now. A lot.

Yuki smiled, putting a little extra sweetness into it, looking up at him from under her eyelashes. She carefully put her cookie back in its little paper bag and brushed powdered sugar off her fingers. "Oh, that's the Federation Room. Not quite so grand. I can show you the way, if you like? It's a little tricky to navigate the mezzanine level."

"That's kind of you. But I wouldn't want to interrupt your coffee break, Miss—"

"Yuki. You can call me Yuki. And it's no problem, sir. I was just about to go and see the Events Manager up that way." That was a lie, but an innocent one. Her friend Melanie was in charge of events at the hotel, and she'd need to tell her all about this man. They always alerted each other to the hot guests, purely for ogling purposes. Being overly friendly or dating the guests was *verboten* by their stricty-pants German hotel manager, Mr Heyer.

"Ah, well. In that case I'd be delighted to have a guide, Miss Yuki. I'm Declan, by the way. Declan Moriarty." He extended his right hand, and she could have fainted with shock. Guests didn't shake hands with staff. But she took his hand, because of course she wanted to touch him.

It was a mistake because he was too sexy. She reached out and shook his hand, or rather he enveloped her small hand totally in his grasp. The heat of his skin was startling, and she bit the inside of her lip to stop a gasp escaping. Tiny ripples of some mysterious energy passed between them, heating her skin and sending prickles of awareness through her whole body. Like static electricity. It certainly felt like every hair on her body was standing on end.

Yuki shivered, although it was far from cold in the Aussie summer. "Mr Moriarty."

He gripped her hand and pumped it a couple more times, grinning at her like the Cheshire cat. "You can call me Declan".

"Declan." She nodded, feeling like Alice descending into another world, a backwards world where up was down, as her stomach had dropped through a virtual rabbit hole.

She let go of his hand and stuffed her cookie in her purse. "Please, follow me."

⸻

The girl called Yuki, a stunning wee lass, rose from her chair under the Christmas tree. She had been sitting there serene as a princess, or an angel, lit up and shining with a silvery glow about her. Declan had been drawn to her, couldn't resist talking to her.

Now she walked away from him at an impressive pace for someone in a skinny dress and heels. He almost yelled at her to slow down, but then...he might have scared her. He was a hotel guest after all, and she worked there. Just trying to do her job.

Her little black dress with the white accents told him she was staff, though he had been at the hotel a few days and hadn't seen her around before. She wiggled her way through the foyer, and he stared after her for a few moments, then half-jogged to catch up. He shouldn't flirt or banter with her. No, definitely not. Pretty as she was...

She stopped and flicked her long shiny black ponytail over her shoulder, glancing his way. "Are you coming, sir?"

Oh, but those words out of her pretty lips were a temptation to play. "Yuki, my dear. I'm simply admiring your athleticism. You practically hurdled that chair to get away from me." Not flirting at all. "Give a poor, short legged Irish man a chance." He pressed his hand to his heart.

Her lips twitched. "Short legged? You have about half a metre on me."

He shrugged. "True, but I don't have your gazelle-like grace. Or would you prefer, a flamingo?" This time she did giggle. The sound was delightful. "Your laugh is like heavenly music". He crossed the floor to catch up to her.

"Um, thank you." She shook her head. "This way." She gestured to a small ramp and a flight of stairs tucked away in a corner.

They walked up the stairs, Yuki ahead of him. "I haven't stayed in this hotel before, but I think I like it more than the Sydney hotel."

"Really? The Sydney Harbour views are amazing though. Well, I think so."

Declan nodded, pausing at the landing where she'd stopped. "Melbourne is my favourite place in Australia though. It's not just the coffee, to be fair, Dublin has good coffee too. I like the people here. More friendly. Genuine."

Yuki beamed at him. "That's exactly what I think. But don't tell my manager. He used to run the Sydney hotel." Yuki continued up the stairs, and he followed.

"Is that so?" He'd met Mr Heyer and hadn't been blown away by his friendliness. He talked down to his staff, and that was something Declan couldn't abide.

A minute later, Yuki directed him to the Grand Ballroom, at the top of the stairs and to the right, through a large sunlit atrium. "I'll be on the reception desk this afternoon if you need anything else, sir."

"Thanks again. And it's Declan."

"Right. See you later, Declan." She ducked her head, and he could have sworn he saw a hint of blush cross her cheek.

The delightful Yuki would be at reception? Then he'd be sure to pay her a visit. He watched her walk away, swaying as she went in her snug little dress. Great legs, even better arse. Petite, and pretty. So very pretty.

"Melanie?" Yuki skidded round the corner into the events office and knocked on her friend's office door. "Mel?"

The door opened, but Melanie had a phone plastered to her ear and pressed her index finger to her lips, signally for Yuki to hush.

"Yes, absolutely. I'll confirm the seating arrangements with the dinner crew and let you know." Melanie gestured for Yuki to come in and sit down. "Okay, thanks very much." She ended the call and sat on the edge of her desk.

Melanie tossed her brown curly hair back and her face positively glowed. "Charity dinner dance for three hundred all confirmed for New Year's Eve. Yes!" She punched the air, then smiled so wide she was almost as toothy as Declan. Almost. "Nailed it, my friend. Now what's going on with you?"

"Um...phew." Yuki crossed her legs in the aqua armchair in the corner of the office, then fanned her face with her hand. She was a little warm, no denying it. "I just met probably the most handsome man on the face of the earth, he shook my hand, and now I'm sweating."

Melanie raised a perfectly arched eyebrow. "Well now. Details please."

Yuki groaned. "He's a guest! Declan Moriarty... Dark wavy hair, eyes like the Pacific Ocean, tall and with this gorgeous smile."

Melanie nodded. "Oooooh. Good, good. He's with the IT conference that's here this week. He owns a hot new start-up. One of the youngest CEOs here, apparently. Not ideal he's a guest, but never mind."

Yuki leaned forward, whispering the most important fact. "And he's Irish!"

Melanie gasped, then covered her mouth with her hand. "Oh no. Did you pee your pants when he spoke to you?"

Yuki rolled her eyes. "Shut up! Okay, nearly. His accent is just soooo cute!"

Giggling, Melanie stood and waggled her finger at Yuki. Dressed in her severe grey suit, she looked like a school head-mistress except for her wild curls, bouncing as she moved. "Yuki Yamimoto, I demand that you flirt with this man, and have some actual fun. You've been far too down in the dumps lately."

Yuki sighed, then opened her purse and found her cookie, and unwrapped it. "I know. It's because I'm waiting to find out about that job. It's been a whole month." She jammed the cookie in her mouth and ate it in two bites.

"I know, the flight attendant job would be awesome, even though I'd miss you. But you can't put your whole life on hold, waiting, just in case you get it."

Yuki finished chewing. "You're right. I know you're right. I can't seem to help wanting things I can't have."

Melanie sighed now and sat next to her on the arm of Yuki's chair. "You can have anything you want. You're young, beautiful..." Yuki snorted. "You are beautiful, believe me, Miss Hottie McTottie. More importantly, you're smart. Opportunity will come, and you'll be ready. But in the meantime..."

"Have some fun." She nodded. It was good advice. Melanie was wise, and more experienced than Yuki, in terms of men and life in general. Not to mention, she had a proper career.

Yuki wanted adventure, a life full of excitement. Maybe meeting Declan was a sign of good things coming her way.

"By the way," Melanie said with a teasing note in her voice, "Mr Meyer won't be here for the rest of this week. I heard he'll be in Sydney until after Christmas. If you were to say, flirt with a guest, he wouldn't even know. If you happened to go out with a certain Irishman, what's the worst that could happen?"

Yuki bit her lip. Right. She had a new Christmas wish list and Declan Moriarty was right at the top.

Chapter Two

Grand Ballroom, The Palladian Hotel

The keynote speaker on IT security was a shockingly boring American man, droning on for hours about denial of service attacks and hacking, which was a potentially interesting topic. He cracked a 'joke' about back-door entry being kind of sexy, and it was all Declan could do to stop himself heckling the man, to tell him to get the hell off the stage, like he was at a comedy club. But he needn't have bothered when the entertainment came busting in the door, uninvited.

A noise like...sleigh bells rang out, and Declan turned his head along with hundreds of other delegates. Searching for the source of the jingling, not to mention doors banging, he craned his neck to check out the ballroom's side doors, standing wide open. He saw a flash of red, a white beard, and yes, it certainly looked like Santa Claus.

"Ho, ho, ho!" A booming voice rang out. It sounded like Santa Claus, too. What was going on?

Declan stood, ignoring the frowns from a sea of men and women in grey and navy suits, and he pushed his way through the row of seats and out into the aisle. The seats were set up theatre style, and he could easily escape through a side door near the coffee station. Striding out of the ballroom door, he stopped in his tracks at a ridiculous sight.

Santa sat in one corner of the large space, on a golden throne no less. A pile of presents sat beside him, along with Mrs Claus and a few elves in full costumes. A photographer had set up his equipment for photos with Santa, complete with North Pole signs. So, IT conference delegates could have a photo with Santa on their tea break? That wasn't even the most ridiculous thing.

He stuck out his hand, blinked several times, not quite believing what he saw. Tiny flakes of white fluttered through the air. Cold, damp flakes. It was snowing in the atrium. Inside the hotel. In Australia. In December. Peak summer, in other words. His mouth popped open, and he craned his neck upwards. A snow machine?

He turned round in a circle, staring at the white flakes falling, swirling around him. When he lowered his gaze, he saw Yuki across the large space, spinning in a circle. Her eyes were wide, and she had that joyful expression, a look of wonder, he remembered from Christmas when he was a child.

Without fully realising what he was doing, his feet were in motion and he walked towards her. He found himself face to face with Yuki. Well, she was still a few metres away, but her gaze found his and they connected. He couldn't describe it any other way. Her eyes lit up and her smile spread into a full-fledged grin, and something inside him melted.

He hadn't seen her yesterday afternoon, hadn't had a spare minute between conference sessions and meetings in the Melbourne city office. When he dropped by Reception in the late evening, she wasn't on duty. He ended up asking for extra pillows and went to bed. After two glasses of whiskey and a hot shower, he managed to sleep. And he had dreamed about a petite, raven haired beauty.

"Isn't this amazing?" Yuki whispered, as if it was a secret.

She had come right up to stand beside him, close enough for him to breathe in the scent of her hair, a floral concoction with a hint of coconut. She smelled like a tropical vacation, which was exactly what he needed.

He let his mouth stretch out in a grin. "Aye. Amazing." His gaze drifted to her lips, until she blinked and looked away. He cleared his throat. "But I have to wonder, what about all this slush? It can't be good for the carpet." He lifted his feet, one at a time, inspecting the soles of his now damp leather shoes.

Yuki glanced his way, then around the room. "Oh, that's not good. I doubt if the Events team approved this. I wonder if my friend Melanie knows..."

"Oh no!" A tall, curly haired woman in a grey suit shouted, then screeched to a halt after coming hard around the corner into the space. She pointed up at the snow, then across the room at a certain jolly fella in a red suit. "You! I never agreed to this!" She marched towards the head Santa sitting on his throne. He was clearly on her naughty list.

Yuki stared at her, then glanced at Declan with a crinkle of worry on her forehead. "Um, I think she knows now. This could get ugly." She flipped her ponytail over her shoulder and whispered, "Let's get out of here."

Glancing at her familiar little black dress, he asked, "Aren't you working?"

She shook her head. "I already clocked off for today." Yuki bit her lip, and she was a perfect mix of sweet and tempting. Nervous though, if he was guessing.

He didn't need to be asked twice. "After you." He gestured for her to take the lead, and he followed Yuki, sidestepping piles of wrapped presents in one corner.

They made their way to the nearest elevator. Yuki pressed the Down button, and they stood waiting in silence. Well, the woman he assumed was Melanie was shouting about contracts and property damage in the background, while *All I Want For Christmas Is You* played cheerily on through the sound system. But he and Yuki didn't say a word, just shared a look that was half silent laughter, half confusion. She pressed her lips together, he cleared his throat and hummed along with the song.

The elevator doors opened with a *ping*, and they both stepped in, keeping a careful few paces distance. There were two other people in the car, one staff member from house-keeping, the other a guest in touristy shorts and t-shirt. Yuki politely nodded to the guest and said, "Good afternoon."

Declan didn't know why exactly, but he kept his mouth firmly closed. Yuki was different with other people around, more reserved. This may not have meant anything, but to him it was a sign. She was interested in him. Probably. He hoped so.

He chanced a sideways look at her, and she was watching the lights of the elevator's display change from M for Mezzanine, to R for Reception. The doors opened and the other two people got out.

When the doors closed again, Yuki turned his way and smiled, her cheeks touched with pink. She spoke softly, keeping her eyes on him. "I was going to ask Melanie if she wanted to come with me to a Christmas market. I don't suppose you would—"

"I'd love to."

"Oh, good." She licked her lower lip with the tip of her tongue and he almost had an aneurysm.

His face heated, he lost his train of thought. Was there a word for awkward anticipation? *Awkipation*? He was bursting full of it.

The elevator light changed to LG for Lower Ground floor, and she stepped forward, so he placed his hand in the small of her back, just for a moment. Yuki's soft inhale of breath was music to his affection-deprived ears. How long had it been since a woman wanted to spend time with him, to hang out? Too long.

They headed out to the street, together. And he thanked his lucky stars.

Christmas Market
Southbank, Melbourne

Yuki didn't know if she'd lost her mind, or if she'd finally found her dating mojo once and for all. She had asked out a man, a deliciously sexy man, and he'd come with her. Just like that!

They walked side by side along the south bank of the Yarra River, the sun sparkling on the water giving it a magical look, not the murky brown river of sludge on show in winter. A river cruise boat floated by, filled with people dressed in fancy clothes, drinking champagne. An office Christmas party, probably.

Skyscrapers of the city centre and the stunning older buildings like Flinders Street Station were just across the water, but here it was Christmas land. Market stalls lined one side of the pedestrian pathway, baubles and sprigs of pine tree hung from lamp posts. Families and couples wandered through the market, picking up handmade gifts and eating treats from other stalls and food trucks. The sound of festive songs played by a brass band, floated on the breeze from the other end of the market.

Declan sighed, a satisfied sound that made her want to ask him what he was thinking, or kiss him. "This is a pretty spot,

Miss Yuki. I like Melbourne. It reminds me of Dublin, to be honest. But the weather is better here, of course."

Yuki giggled like a school girl. This man affected like that, she felt lighter, carefree. "The weather in Melbourne is revolting most of the year. Rainy drizzle, freezing cold wind and grey skies."

"It really is like Dublin, then."

She snort-laughed this time, and she would have been embarrassed except he grinned, his whole face lighting up. He also took her arm in an old-fashioned gentlemanly way. The way it made her feel wasn't so innocent. Her whole body heated —the sun had nothing on the way Declan had her glowing.

Yuki kept walking and caught a glance of a popular stall. "Oh, look at the crystals over there." They steered through a bunch of people to take a closer look at a stall filled with glittering jewels, Swarovski crystals and semi-precious stones.

The jewellery wasn't too expensive, but so pretty that she *ooohed* and *aahhed* over more than one piece. She touched a string of transparent crystals with a large silver pendant at the end.

"It's gorgeous, but I couldn't possibly justify it." Very sensible. She was trying to save money after all. But it was sad to leave it there, unloved and unbought.

"Wrap it up, please." Declan's voice was deep and sure from her left side. She turned to him, mouth agape. "You can't just go around buying me necklaces, willy nilly!"

His lips tipped up at the corners. "Willy nilly? Aye, I think you'll find I can, even higgeldy piggeldy. Consider it an early Christmas gift." He winked at the older woman who ran the stall, a stunning silk headscarf wrapped around her head. "I'll have one of these bracelets for my Mam too."

The stall holder wrapped his purchases and offered her holiday wishes, and Yuki stood there like she'd been frozen to the spot. Buying her presents? Already? In the same breath as buying things for his mother...this could be something. Something real. Maybe.

She sneakily looked at him side-on while he chatted away in that oh-so-charming accent. He was too good to be true. She took a sip from her water bottle, biding her time while her mind performed triple backflip gymnastics.

He was from another country. He'd be leaving soon. Anyway, he probably didn't even fancy her. He was only being polite. She couldn't go falling for him...

Declan handed her the little parcel, and murmured, right near her ear, "Here, Miss Yuki. A little something to stuff in your stocking."

She laughed, and choked. Water exploded from her lips. The horror! She ducked her head, but Declan moved closer, touching her lips with his fingertip. She tipped her head up to meet his eyes, and there was A Moment. His thumb brushed her lower lip, wiping off drops of water, and she could have sworn her heart stopped.

"There now." Declan cleared his throat and stepped away from her. "Right. Right! Should we get something to eat?"

Oh no. Had she scared him off with her sheer silliness?

Oh, give me strength. Declan raised his eyes to invisible higher powers and wished for the billionth time he was as smooth as Cary Grant in an old movie. Then again, Cary did do a few bumbling comedy scenes, and women still liked him, so maybe all hope wasn't lost. And his real name was Archibald, a million times worse than Declan.

They walked through the crowd of shoppers, Yuki to his right. She'd gone quiet. He didn't know what to make of it. It was not his usual style to hit on women he'd only just met. Not at all.

When he'd met Kendra, his ex, his first thought was, nice woman, capable, she probably wouldn't pressure him to be romantic. They worked together, and they got along fine. They didn't go on a real date for at least a month. Now that he thought about it, that wasn't a good sign.

Looking back, their relationship was probably doomed. There was never a real spark.

Looking at Yuki, there were sparks enough to set off a spectacular New Year's Eve fireworks show.

"What about a taco?" Yuki had stopped walking and was staring at the chalkboard menu outside a food truck. The whole space was decorated with fairy lights and strings of silver stars, fully pimped-out for the holiday season.

"Sure, sounds good." Declan ordered a taco with interesting local ingredients – Barramundi fish and lemon myrtle mayo, who knew that was a thing? – with an Aussie beer on the side. He carried his and Yuki's drinks and found them a table on the tiny lawn by the riverside.

When she sat beside him, instead of opposite, he couldn't think for a few seconds. This was a date now, right? He was almost sure. He undid the first two buttons of his shirt and rolled up his sleeves. He was hotly aware of Yuki's eyes on him as he moved.

She breathed out, then quickly said, "This is the best date I've been on in ages." She paused, then laughed lightly. "Was that a weird thing to say?"

His laugh came out of nowhere, right from his gut. "Ha! I don't think so, but I'm hardly an arbiter of normal-ness. I am a tech nerd. I rarely leave my cave."

Yuki tipped her head to one side, studying his face. "I don't think that's true. You own a company, right? I'm sure you get out and about. Women are probably falling all over you, looking like..." She waved her hand vaguely in front of him, gesturing from his head to toes.

He tried not to scrunch up his face into a frown, but probably failed. "Looking like what exactly? An Irish hipster doofus?"

Her laugh caught him off guard, like a peal of silver bells. "No, you dag. I meant, all handsome and gorgeous. Full of Irish charm too."

His face nearly split in half from the stupid grin no doubt taking over his face. She thought he was handsome and gorgeous. And charming? Well, his luck was changing. "Coming from a stunningly gorgeous girl, such as yourself, I'll take that as a huge compliment."

Now Yuki ducked and hid her face from him, looking out across the river at the city view. But he spotted the corner of her smile, the little dimple in her cheek. "But do you have women falling all over you? I've been burned before by men who pretended to be single. Especially when they're on holidays."

He nodded. Men could be arseholes, it was undoubtedly true. "Ah, I'm definitely single. I was engaged, but it ended over six months ago. Kendra and I didn't gel as a couple. Unfortunately, I have to see her tomorrow. She works at our Melbourne office now."

When Yuki turned back to meet his eyes, she looked worried. An adorable little line had formed in the spot between her eyebrows. "You broke off your engagement? What happened?"

His so-called friend had happened. Matthias was never blackening his doorstep again, after his part in ending Declan's relationship and leading their business down the wrong path.

He shrugged. That part of his life was over, so no harm talking about it. "Kendra wasn't quite as committed to the idea of monogamy as I was. Plus, my former friend and business partner was apparently better for her than I was, since I'm so old fashioned and stuck in my ways, insisting on complete honesty."

"Wow."

"Yeah. It is what it is. But I could have done without seeing my friend shagging my fiancée in my bed, two days before my wedding."

Yuki gritted her teeth, then plonked her beer down hard on the table. "What complete arseholes. I'd say you're better off without either of them."

"My thoughts exactly." Declan took a long swig of his beer. He never talked about that whole disaster, let alone to someone he'd only just met. But it felt good to get it out there, with Yuki.

A waitress arrived with their tacos, and as they ate they made small talk, no more heavy stuff. Decan's mind ticked over. He had to decide what to do.

Yuki was a real temptation. But was he ready to open himself up again with a woman? Kendra had ripped him right open with her style of makeshift open-heart surgery. He'd only just managed to stitch himself together.

He glanced across at Yuki to find her monstering a taco and licking her lips. "Oh. My. God. This taco is amaaaazing."

She licked her lips again, and he groaned before he could stop himself.

"What?"

She was completely oblivious to how sexy she was. He shook his head. "Nothing. Enjoy your taco. I have to get back to the hotel. Work to do." He stood too quickly, awkward as hell, bumping his knee on the table leg.

"Oh. Will I see you tomorrow?"

His first instinct was to say no, to say goodbye to her. But his instincts sucked lately. He'd have to give it some thought. "Maybe. I have the office Christmas party, but I'll be around later."

Yuki smiled, a ray of sunshine. "Great. I'll be at Reception if you need me."

He waved and walked away, not sure if the lightness in his body was simply because of Yuki, or the odd feeling of being free to do what he wanted for a change. Probably both. He'd definitely give it some thought.

Chapter Three

Palladian Hotel

For the past two days, Yuki's favourite guest had been flirting and hitting her with his high-beam super-smile in between his business meetings. Declan was making her wish for things that until a few days ago, seemed impossible.

Now he wandered into the hotel and he looked completely worn out. His rumpled wavy dark hair and scowl said his company's Christmas party hadn't been at all joyful. Poor Declan.

Tapping her foot where she stood behind the hotel reception desk in her low-heeled pumps, she sighed. Hotel guests were off limits to staff fraternizing. It was a crying shame, because she could see herself fraternizing all over him, in a naughty way. She should say no, if Declan flirted with her again or if he actually asked her out. He had been in fine form earlier, calling her "an afternoon delight" and "the angel of hotel reception".

Declan was obviously rich, handsome in a cheeky, wavy haired, blue eyed, wide shouldered kind of way, like a male model who dabbled in professional rugby and maybe romantic poetry. Smart as a whip, too. He was completely out of her league, not to mention one hundred percent off limits.

Still, she couldn't deny his delicious Irish accent had her melting into a puddle whenever he opened his mouth. Long story short, he was someone she should treat with deference, respect and absolutely not spill her overflowing store of bubbling lust over him. She could lose her job.

He sauntered up to the desk, taking his sweet time, grinning at her like a sexy loon when he spotted her watching him. Honestly, he was making it difficult to be good. Yuki tapped her fingertips on the desk. Only good little hotel staffers got Christmas bonuses. She would need the money when she (fingers crossed) moved to London in the new year.

On the other hand, she had to remember, she was no longer the type of girl to say no at all, as of exactly a week ago. Yuki had decided to lead a more adventurous life. To follow her heart, to listen to the inner voice that was whispering to her to take more chances, to expand her horizons... and to get properly laid. She would say yes, to every opportunity.

She forced her eyes away from him and pretended to check some bookings on the computer monitor.

"Good evening, Mr Moriarty," she began, and flicked her eyes up to meet his, a good six inches above her own. He was standing very close, leaning right up against the marble countertop. She sucked in a breath at the expression in his sapphire blue eyes. There was an unspoken challenge there, and undeniable heat.

"Good evening yourself, Miss Yuki. Now what would a gorgeous girl such as yourself be doing working on the eve of Christmas Eve?"

She kept her voice low. "Oh, you know. Working for The Man, earning my Christmas bonus." She bit her lip to stop herself talking.

No way did he know what it was like, working for The

Man. He was The Man. His tech company was one of the most successful start-ups in Ireland, or so she'd read. She now knew he had an Asia Pacific office in Melbourne too. He was only twenty-seven and had a staff of over one hundred people.

He raised one dark eyebrow, somehow setting his eyes to extra sparkly mode. "Ah, is that so? I wouldn't want to stand between a woman and her Christmas bonus. That could be bad. Cursed. It would be worse than breaking up a wedding, which I've had occasion to do, would you believe?"

Yuki pressed her lips together since she was in danger of giggling. "Ignore me, please. It's been a long week. The national department store Santa convention is in town and they drink a surprising amount of egg nog and whiskey, even at the breakfast buffet."

Her colleague, Carlos, snorted from where he stood at the bag check in area, a couple of metres away. He muttered something like, "True dat." She turned and gave him her best evil-eyed look. Carlos shook his head and backed away, ready to go on his break.

Yuki smiled at Declan, giving her handsome guest her full attention again. "My apologies, sir. What can I do for you this evening?"

The question apparently amused him. He flashed her a winning smile, all the more adorable because of the slightest gap between his front teeth. "To be honest, Yuki, my Christmas eve-eve plans have rather fallen flat. I was hoping you could recommend a good Irish pub or Australian type drinking establishment not too far away. I'd prefer no egg nog if at all possible."

She tapped at her computer screen. Angling it to show him some photos, she said, "Many of our guests like the Kookaburra Klub, only a block away."

He tilted his head, studying the photos. "Ah, bless. There's fake Kookaburras on the walls. No, I was thinking of a place you might personally recommend. Maybe somewhere you'd go after work."

Yuki nodded, catching his eye. She thought she'd caught his meaning too. "Let's see. When I finish work around midnight, like tonight, I sometimes Uber it to St Kilda and go to the Wheel and Barrow. It's a proper pub, beer on tap, live music, all that. Some friends of mine are in a band. They're playing tonight. Hard Candy."

She'd put it out there, sneakily dropped a big old hint that she'd be there later, and he could join her if he wanted to. No problem if he didn't mean what she thought he'd meant. She'd just sulk into her artisan pilsner and listen to the band.

"Thank you, Ms Yuki. I might change out of this cursed suit and head out there soon." He nodded, loosened his burgundy silk tie, and stared at her for a good half a minute. He hesitated, mouth open as if he was about to say something important. "Grand. Have a good night."

"Good evening, sir."

Yuki took a deep breath and watched him walk away, towards the bank of elevators on the east side of the hotel.

Right. She checked the time on her computer. It was already after eleven P.M. Not long until her shift was over. She exhaled and pressed a hand to her chest. Her heart was going a mile a minute, and all he'd done was talk to her.

She would have to pace herself or she might pass out before the clock ticked over to midnight. Christmas Eve.

Declan ended the phone call after about forty long minutes and tossed his phone on the bed. He hadn't needed that call. Not now, not tonight. He scrubbed his hands through his hair, pacing his hotel suite like a trapped tiger in a cage.

Jon was a trustworthy man. His new second-in-command in the Irish office was both a lawyer and a systems architect. If Jon said the company had invested in the wrong technology and was sinking, Declan believed him. They had better patch the hole in the ship's hull or otherwise get a whole lot of life preservers. They would work out a plan, a new direction.

But first, he had a date. At least he thought so. Damn, was he really doing this?

Declan searched through his suitcase and the wardrobe in his hotel suite, looking for something to wear that wouldn't make him look like an absolute tool. All business clothes.

"Bloody stupid. Suits should be banned," he muttered as he pulled out the drawers in the bureau.

He couldn't go to a local pub dressed like a typical IT guy, or he may as well wear a 'Kick Me' sign. But wait… His old friend Gabriel had given him a surf brand shirt when they'd caught up at Bells Beach last week. With his black jeans and trainers, that would do.

He quickly showered and changed, leaving his hair damp to curl as it pleased. Would Yuki like him this way? Out of his usual corporate uniform? She'd been in uniform all week, just like him.

Yuki, the gorgeous girl at the hotel's front desk. So friendly, so sweet. Her slight Australian accent, her long elegant neck with the little silver necklace she wore, and shiny hair black as midnight, always up in a sleek ponytail. Mostly it was her stunning wide eyes that had him almost lost for words. That wasn't like him at all. His old man often said Declan could talk the hind legs off a donkey. She had been the ultimate distraction from his business in Melbourne this week. And he definitely needed a distraction.

His ex-fiancée Kendra might have been a smart woman, a brilliant programmer, but as Chief Operating Officer she'd run the Asia Pacific arm of the company into the ground. He'd had to reassign her to another project, and he couldn't pretend it was a promotion. Hell of a way to ruin the office Christmas party, making that little announcement.

He'd got out of there as soon as possible, wishing Kendra well on his way out, though it half-killed him to do it. He could still feel the way she'd glared daggers at his back. He had more than enough anger to fire back at her if he chose. She'd been the one to cheat on him after all. He'd dodged a bullet there.

He nodded at his reflection in the bathroom mirror, running his fingers over the rough stubble along his jaw. "You can do this. Flirt with a pretty girl. Drink a few beers. Have a laugh. Pretend that the universe doesn't hate you, and your whole life didn't fall in the cosmic toilet this year."

He grabbed his phone and wallet, and headed out of the hotel, into the humid summer night to meet his taxi. And to meet the unlikely girl who had taken hold of his imagination, even his dreams.

Why did he have a feeling he was about to do something monumentally stupid? Ah well, it wouldn't be the first time.

Chapter Four

Yuki stared into her beer, watching the swirl of foam on the surface and trying to find pictures in it, as if she was reading tea leaves in a porcelain cup. The beer wasn't even cold anymore. She wouldn't drink it warm, like an Englishman, or a psycho.

She blocked out the noise of punters arguing at the bar, and the frenetic thud of drums from the warm-up band. She settled back in the Reserved booth seat she'd found near the back of the band room. There was a silver Christmas tree balanced on the top of the booth, and she watched the string of lights wrapped around it flicker in pretty patterns.

She had hurried here from the hotel, thinking Declan Moriarty would be waiting for her. But obviously she was wrong. Clearly he'd changed his mind, or had a better offer. Hopefully it wasn't his ex keeping him busy.

She blocked out that depressing line of thought. Her

friend's band would be on stage soon, and maybe one or two of her hotel co-workers would turn up too. The night didn't have to be a total write-off.

"Hello, Miss Yuki." The deep voice, the delectable Irish accent made her gasp. She flicked her head around to where he stood, just to her right.

"If it isn't the most beautiful girl in the world sitting under a Christmas tree. You must be waiting for Santa Claus. Will I do for company in the meantime?" He grinned, and even in the low lighting, his teeth almost glowed white.

Yuki's cheek muscles stretched out in a smile she couldn't contain. "You'll do. Get over here. I mean, please sit down, Mr Moriarty. Sir." She giggled like a fool. She couldn't help it. *He came!*

He shuffled into the booth to sit right beside her, like a couple, not like random strangers. He was only a hand's distance away. "As much as I like it when you call me Sir, I asked you to call me Declan."

"Okay, Declan." Yuki paused to study him. He was simply a beautiful man. Out of his starchy suits, he was even more attractive. More human, more touchable. "I'm glad you came."

"So am I. You look stunning, as always." His eyes traced her body, gaze skimming over her silver shift dress. She shivered. That intense look of his, the depth in his flashing blue eyes, had her filled with anticipation. "Great dress. You look like a movie star."

"Thanks." The dress had done its job. It was probably overkill, but she loved to dress up. And it was Christmas Eve after all. "I was in the mood to celebrate. Christmas bonus, remember. I get paid tomorrow."

He chucked, a sound that resonated low in her abdomen, tugging at muscles she'd almost forgotten she had. Then he raised his right hand and placed it over hers, on the table top. "You're my Christmas bonus, if you don't mind my being cheesy."

She didn't mind, not one cheesy bit. She loved cheese. Her luck was totally changing. His hand was large and warm on hers, and the scent of his aftershave, like the sea breeze in summer with a hint of warm spice, wrapped around her.

"I've never been anyone's Christmas bonus before." She took a breath, finding him watching her, focusing on her lips.

Yuki swallowed, her mouth suddenly dry. "I meant to say, back at the hotel, I hoped your work event was okay. You looked so down when you came back tonight."

He tipped his head to one side so a wave of his hair flopped over his forehead. "Ah, it wasn't all merry and bright. Problems with some of our investments, trusting the wrong people, that kind of thing. But I'll sort it out when I get back to Dublin."

She nodded, but something heavy sunk in the pit of her belly. "When do you fly back?"

He sighed, and suddenly he sounded exhausted. "Tomorrow night, late. Sorry, I mean tonight. I have Christmas with my Ma and Da back home. I'll just make it with the time difference."

"So soon?"

Declan threaded his fingers through hers, squeezing her hand. "I know, it's not the best timing." He caught her gaze and there was something there hiding in his eyes, a sadness that surprised her.

Yuki let go of his hand and raised hers to touch the adorable scruff on his jaw. "So? That means we have to pack a lot of fun into one day."

Then she leaned in, gently pressing her mouth to his, and tasted his lips. Delicious man. She kissed him like this was her last ever kiss, and tonight was the end of the world.

Honestly, if the world was ending, she intended to go out with a bang.

Declan groaned as Yuki, this beautiful girl, pressed her mouth to his. She tasted of fruity lip gloss, mango maybe. It was officially his favourite flavour in the whole world. He leaned in to wrap his arm around her shoulders, pulling her body close to him. He licked across her lower lip and she opened for him, so he took the kiss deeper.

This time it was her turn to groan, a small sound of surrender. The sound unlocked something inside him, some vault he'd hidden away filled with pain and loneliness. He didn't feel any of that with Yuki. It was all engulfing heat. Attraction. An irresistible pull towards her.

He tilted his head, kissed the side of her mouth, then across her cheek. He wanted her, so much, but this wasn't the place. He ran his fingers through her loose hair, a silk curtain, smooth against his fingers.

"Yuki." He let his forehead rest against hers. "Where did you come from?"

"Declan. I came from Swanston Street, in an Uber." She beamed at him, her eyes sparkling with laughter.

He chuckled. "I meant, how did I happen to meet you, all the way across the world?"

"Luck."

"The luck of the Irish?"

Her lips lifted up into a sweet smile. "Something like that."

A scraping sound, a chair being dragged over concrete, had him glancing over Yuki's shoulder. A lanky blonde fellow dressed in a flannel shirt and ripped jeans had pulled his chair right up to theirs, too close for his liking.

"This is a great pub. Great vibe. Good to be back." The words brought Declan halfway back to earth. The man spoke again, watching Yuki far too closely. "Hey Yuki, who's your friend?"

She pulled away from Declan, straightening her spine. "Hi Glenn. This is Declan, visiting from Ireland. Declan, Glenn's in my friend's band. He plays guitar."

"Aren't I your friend too?"

Yuki's posture stiffened. "Um, sure. Where's Blair?"

"She's on her way. Getting her mics and stuff out of the van."

A long-suffering sigh from Yuki told Declan exactly what she thought of this guy. "By herself? Shouldn't you help her with that?"

Glenn shrugged, apparently clueless. "Oh, yeah. Probably. I'll be right back." He loped off, heading in the direction of a side exit.

Declan asked a careful question, to gauge Yuki's reaction. "Not your favourite person?"

Yuki turned to him and whispered, "Glenn is Exhibit A in the case of me versus arseholes I used to date."

"Ah." Declan did not want to talk about Glenn The Arsehole Ex. He tried for a change of subject. "So, your friend Blair, is she a singer?"

"Oh yes, and a songwriter. She's so talented, one of those people who just lights up a room, you know?"

He touched Yuki's face, stroking the soft skin of her cheek. "Aye, I know someone like that." Declan watched the compliment sink in, Yuki's eyes sparkling in the low lighting.

This night, with this girl, it could be one of those times he'd always remember. A little festive magic was in the air. He wanted her, wanted to kiss her again. He hoped she felt the same.

‧｡･ﾟ

An hour later, the band was on stage, they'd had a couple of drinks and Yuki was having the best time. Declan was by her side as they danced along to the music near the front of the stage. He had surprisingly good moves for an IT guy. She glanced his way and nearly lost her balance, but he grabbed her hips with his big strong hands. She nearly swooned. When he let her go, she missed his touch like her next breath.

Blair was killing it tonight. In her gold mini dress and combat boots, platinum blonde pixie haircut and with a scarlet guitar strapped to her, she was a rock goddess. Her voice was brilliant too. She belted out the Ladyhawke tune, *Magic,* the words floating over the crowd like a spell. A song about a man who lived over the Atlantic, but maybe if they were together, it could be magic. For a lifetime.

Yuki soaked in the scene. The heat and noise of the crowd faded as Declan took her hand. She reached up, her other hand on the nape of his neck. He leaned down and she kissed him, just a brief touch of lips, but enough to cause a whoosh of a flame to ignite inside her.

The band finished up the song with a string of thank yous, and Blair said, "Happy Christmas Eve, Melbourne." The crowd erupted in woops and yelling. She passed a mic to Glenn, who had been leaning slouchily near the drum kit.

He started strumming his guitar, then said, "This song's for Yuki."

A gasp left her mouth in a rush, and she crossed her arms under her breasts. She recognised the start of the song, *Under The Milky Way* by The Church, one of her all time favourites. Glenn wouldn't ruin it for her. No way.

"Declan, do you mind if we get some fresh air?" She turned to find him watching her already, his eyes narrowed a little.

"No problem. This way." He ushered her through the crowd to the side of the stage, behind some massive speakers.

A side door with a glowing green Exit sign marked the way out.

In less than a minute, they stumbled out of the heat and noise into fresh air, cooler than Yuki had been expecting. They were in a small courtyard dotted with a few cafe tables, strung with fairy lights overhead, stars shimmering far above in the summer sky.

The courtyard was empty and fenced off from a side street. A few smokers stood on the other side of the fence, taking in low voices. The music from inside the pub followed them, a haunting song that always gave her shivers. Goosebumps prickled her bare arms.

Declan took her hand again and pulled her towards him. "Are you okay?"

She nodded, watching for Declan's reaction. "Yeah. But Glenn has some balls dedicating a song to me. Last time I saw him, we had been hanging out at my apartment, and he told me he was going out for beer. Next thing I heard, he was in Sydney recording an album with some other band, living with some other girl. That was months ago."

His face went stony. A muscle in his jaw twitched. "He just up and left?"

"Uh huh. But I don't want to spend any more time talking about him."

Declan's expression shifted to a half smile. "In that case, will you dance with me?"

Her heart stuttered at the lines etched on his forehead, the questioning look he gave her, half expectation, half anxiety.

"Yes". Of course, the answer was yes.

She stepped forward and almost fell against him, his arms wrapped around her, with her head resting against his chest. They swayed together, bodies in sync with the music. Yuki's heart picked up speed when Declan tipped her chin up with his fingertips, staring down at her with unfathomably deep blue eyes.

"Hey, you."

He kissed her, and all thoughts rushed out of her head. She was on her tiptoes, reaching for him, hands around the back of his neck, when he lifted her up and spun them around. He deepened the kiss, sliding his tongue against hers, tasting her. Her head spun with the dizzy sensation, and her little handbag fell to the ground with a thump.

One of his hands held her up, under her butt, the other roamed over her body. She moved against him, feeling his hardness pressed against her, the heat of him searing her skin through her thin dress.

He let her down, but her legs were shaky. She clung to him, and if her hand ended up under his shirt, stroking his flat stomach, so what? He kissed down her throat, his hand cupping the underside of her breast, now his thumb stroked back and forth across her hard nipple, while he licked the shell of her ear. She ached. God, she ached for him.

He took her mouth again, more possessive this time. Oh, *wow*. The man could kiss. How lucky could she get?

Before she knew what was happening, the song had finished and the band started playing a stupidly loud version of some Kings of Leon song. They broke apart, watching each other, both breathing heavily. His shirt was half unbuttoned where she'd tried to get at more of skin. A nice V of hair on his chest taunted her, tempted her to touch.

"Stay with me tonight?" His voice was gruff.

Yuki bit her lip. "At the hotel?" She hesitated, but only because of stupid rules. "It's not really allowed."

He shrugged, one eyebrow lifted. "Want to be a little bit naughty?"

Oh God, he was cute. She ran her hand over his jaw again, planting a fairy kiss on his mouth. "Mmmm. And a little bit nice, I hope. Let's go."

Chapter Five

The Palladian Hotel
Three A.M. on Christmas Eve

Sneaking into the hotel like a thief in the middle of the night, where he was a lawful paying guest, wasn't something Declan had on his Christmas bingo card. But with Yuki holding his hand, it was a hell of a lot of fun. Sprinting past Reception without being seen was going to be the tricky part.

They stood behind a marble column right inside the hotel's front entrance, Yuki's body hidden from view behind him. The concierge desk was empty, closed down for the night, and the lighting in the foyer was dimmed.

Yuki swivelled this way and that, checking out the scene. She whispered, "I think we could sneak over to the elevators by the restaurant, but we'd need to be quick."

"Okay. On the count of three…"

But sleigh bells jingled from outside, someone chuckled, and a whole lot of footsteps echoed down the empty street. Someone was singing *Santa Claus is Coming To Town*.

Declan took a deep breath, then tugged on Yuki's arm. "Wait. Listen."

They both turned and stared out the large plate glass windows facing the street. Santas were coming. A whole group of them, walking, stumbling to the hotel's entrance. They had to be drunk. The singing was awful.

One of the Santas swiped a key card and the front doors swooshed open. And in they danced, all dressed up in full red and white regalia. Declan whipped his head around. He blinked at Yuki, whose mouth was hanging open. What could only be described as a conga line of Santas came dancing right past them, into the foyer.

He and Yuki glanced at each other again. He nudged her arm, then nodded in the direction of the elevator. He held up his hand, waiting for the oblivious Santas to dance past their position, singing *Frosty The Snowman* now. He nodded again, then mouthed: *three, two, one*. He went first.

They ran, along one wall, like their pants were on fire. Maybe they were, so to speak, because he'd never wanted anything more than to get Yuki into his bed. Behind him, Yuki let out a yelping noise, and he turned to find her rubbing her head, and a hatless Santa rubbing his.

"He slammed right into me," she stage-whispered in Declan's direction.

Santa was unsteady on his feet. He pointed at Yuki. "Sorry. Wait... You're the nice one from Reception. The one who found me the good whiskey." The man's head turned as if in slow-motion to Declan, giving him the once over. "You sneaking in?"

Declan nodded, craning his neck to see if the night manager had heard all the noise. Ten metres of foyer separated them from Reception, and no one was walking their way. They were safe, for now.

Yuki said, "He's my boyfriend. I'm not supposed to stay here overnight."

Declan's face heated and his grin was probably manic. *Boyfriend?* He liked the sound of that.

The hatless Santa frowned, his stick-on beard flapping on one side. "Bah humbug! Leave it to me." He tapped the side of his nose with one finger.

He dashed over to one of his younger man-in-red-suit friends, grabbed him by the collar and dragged him over. "Give the girl your hat and jacket." The other man shrugged, his eyes unfocused, and mildly confused.

"Yuki. That's my name."

Yuki took the offered costume and quickly put it on over her dress. She swam in it, petite as she was. She tucked her hair into her jacket and adjusted her hat, then caught Declan's eyes. Her dark eyes sparkled with mischief. She was cute as a button, or a fake Mrs Claus on the run from the law.

The first man nodded, saying under his breath, "I'm Brian, but you can call me Kris Kringle." Brian/Kris grabbed his own jacket by the lapels and took it off, handing it to Declan. Declan dressed too, scanning the space for the manager at the same time.

Declan thought he knew the plan now. Pretend to be Santas, blend in. It was just ridiculous enough that it might work, at least at three o'clock in the morning on Christmas Eve.

Brian moved with relative grace for a man who had a naturally Santa-esque frame, moving to push Declan and Yuki into line in front of him. They soon caught up to the rest of the staggering Santas, halfway across the foyer, now singing a rousing rendition of *Rudolph The Red Nosed Reindeer*.

They simply joined in singing, formed a conga line and headed across the large open plan space. Yuki ducked behind Declan, half giggling, half humming. When they were near the elevator, Brian turned and gave Declan the thumbs up.

Declan dashed to the right, holding Yuki's hand, pulling

her with him round the corner to the elevator in a cul-de-sac. He slammed his hand onto the Up button.

In the distance, he heard Brian give a hearty "Ho, ho, ho!", no doubt distracting the manager on the Reception desk.

Declan and Yuki looked into each other's eyes and broke into silent laughter. The elevator car came, and they hopped aboard. No kissing, no touching, Declan was a good boy and kept a polite distance from Yuki at all times. But the tension between them was an invisible force, keeping their eyes on each other. Connected.

Yuki waited, hopping from foot to foot in her heels, as Declan scanned his key card on the electronic lock on the door to the Executive Suite on the twenty fifth floor. The door clicked open, and then they were inside.

The suite's lights clicked on now, only a hazy golden glow from the lamp by the bed and a crack of light from the bathroom. It was a gorgeous room, probably as big as her whole apartment. Silver grey walls and black and white silk bedding said luxury, in a rich-people understated way. But there was a modern crystal chandelier, sparkling in the low light, which set the whole thing off in her humble opinion.

She didn't want to waste any more time. Declan was just ahead of her, tossing his wallet and keys on the wooden side table. He still wearing his Santa jacket. She tugged on his fur-trimmed sleeve, so he turned to face her. Then he grabbed his jacket by the lapels and pulled him closer. She ran her hands over his biceps, stroking him. Then she was trying to get the jacket off, fiddling with Velcro tabs.

Declan huffed out a breath on a half laugh. "Woah, what's the rush?"

Yuki blinked at him. "Are you freaking kidding me? Kiss me already, you great Irish fool."

He grabbed her waist as he chuckled, deep and throaty. "As you wish."

He pressed his lips down upon hers, like she was the rain and he was a parched man in the desert. She squeaked out of the corner of her mouth as he licked across her lower lip, then bit it, gently. Yuki kissed him back, melting into him, closing her eyes against the rush of heat, the ache taking over her body.

She didn't want to rely on her legs to hold her upright, so she jumped on him. It was only logical. He caught her, wrapped her legs around his back and held her there, grinding against her in such a way...she knew he wanted her. And she needed him. Now.

Yuki groaned, breaking their kiss. "Oh my gawwwwd...quick! Take your clothes off."

"Alright, alright." He laughed again, and she felt the reverberation of it under her hands.

She was unbuttoning his shirt, with fumbling, shaking hands. And they were moving. Declan had spun them around and was walking them towards the bed. A second later he let her go and plopped her down on the bed like a sack of potatoes.

"Hey!"

But then she raised her eyes and saw what he was doing. He yanked off his red jacket and pulled his shirt straight over his head, muscles in his stomach and chest tensing and flexing with the action. His hair stood up, waves all gorgeous and messy. He was beautiful. Not thin, built with slabs of corded muscles, dusted in dark hair. A small black tattoo, a Celtic design on his bicep, had her salivating. She wanted to taste his skin, all over. His eyes were wild as he stared down at her.

She ripped off her Santa hat and shook out her hair, then

got rid of her own red jacket, tossing it on the floor. Yuki kept her eyes on Declan, as her pulse thudded in her ears, and between her legs. With a quick move, her silver sheath dress was unzipped and she shimmied it down and off. It slithered off her legs, leaving her in nothing but her black silky bra and underwear.

"Oh, Miss Yuki. Look at you. So gorgeous." He popped open the button on his jeans, and she bit her lip. He toed off his sneakers, kicked them away, then tugged down his jeans. She breathed out at the sight of him, wearing only black boxers.

He came to her, climbing onto the edge of the bed beside her. The first thing he did, literally first, was lean down and kiss her belly button. A flick of his tongue there had her gasping. He ran one big hand down over her underwear, stroking her.

He looked up at her, his eyes in shadow. He pulled aside the fabric and touched her, making her squirm. "Do you want me to kiss you here?"

She leaned back on her elbows, watching him. "Yes, but later. Come here."

He crawled up her body until he lay partly on top of her, still it was an awkward shuffle until he was pressed fully against her. She kissed his chest, the base of his throat, nuzzling there until he groaned and slid the strap of her bra down one shoulder.

Declan pulled down the silk fabric so her breast was exposed, and then his mouth was on her flesh, kissing and sucking her sensitive nipple. In two seconds flat, she had wriggled her bra off and he was kissing her other breast, cupping it with his big hand, teasing her. She was so on edge already, she was panting, the feeling was so intense.

Pressing his lips to her throat, he murmured, "Yuki, I want you."

She nodded, catching her breath. "Me too. Do you have protection?"

He placed a sweet kiss on her cheek. "Wait here, don't move." He climbed off her, dashed over to the table where he'd left his wallet and then he was back again.

Back on the bed, he sat beside her, and she propped herself on her side, watching him. His boxers came off, then the hard length of him sprang up, straining almost against his flat stomach. She swallowed, hard, as he tore open the condom wrapper in his hand, and rolled it over himself in a fluid motion.

When he looked up at her, she simply reached out for him, and then they were together. He peeled off her knickers, and he touched her again, exactly where she was aching. They tangled in a mass of arms and legs, mostly hers, wrapped high around his waist.

He placed kisses down her neck, to her lips, his hands roaming on her body. He slid a hand between them and stroked her, until Yuki was ready and rocking beneath him, trying to get closer. Close as possible.

"Declan, please," she said. She wasn't too proud to beg, especially when it got results.

He gripped her hip and rocked into her, until he slid right inside her. So good. So perfect. Yuki let a full lungful of air gush out of her lips, before biting Declan's shoulder and kissing him. Kissing him. Always kissing him.

Their hips worked, and Yuki surged up to meet Declan, over and over, until she shook with need. He raised himself up on his strong forearms and thrust into her, once, twice, taking her over the edge with him as they floated on a cloud, silver stars falling in the night sky behind her eyelids.

Later, she snuggled in the huge bed next to Declan, who totally hogged the covers. She blinked and opened her eyes, rubbed up against the roughness of his leg hair, and flung her own leg over his.

Declan rolled over and kissed her lips. "Hey, Miss Yuki. I think I'm falling for this girl. Do you think I should tell her? Yes or no?"

Her heart flipped over, doing somersaults. "Yes. Always yes. And you should kiss her. A lot."

His twisted half smile, like he was trying to be serious, was totally adorable. "Noted." He cleared his throat, then said in a dramatic deep voice, "Yuki, I think I'm falling for you."

Yuki let the warm glow spreading through her body show itself on her face, her cheek muscles stretching out with the force of her grin. She snuggled closer to Declan until she could kiss him, tugging his lower lip with her teeth.

He made a noise like, "Hmmmpf" and flipped her onto her back.

Then he was moving down the bed, kissing her belly button again. "A lot of kisses, huh?" He raised his eyebrows before he flipped the sheet over his head and kissed a path all the way down, to exactly where she wanted him.

"Oh, Declan!"

Chapter Six

Declan was usually up with the birds, whether he liked it or not. Not this morning though. He'd slept like a bear hibernating for the winter. Only his phone woke him up, rousing the drowsy and cranky bear. Whoever it was, making him get out of bed while Yuki was still in it, warm and soft, cuddling up to him, better be warned. He was in a mood. It stopped ringing.

He grabbed his phone off the bedside table, rolling out of bed and crossing the room in his boxers to stand near the windows. Three missed calls, all from Kendra. Oh hell. It rang again in his hand.

"Ah, shit." He took the call, trying not to completely lose his cool. "Declan."

"Well, hello. I've been trying to call for ages. What on earth are you doing?"

Declan sighed, grabbing a clean t-shirt from his suitcase

and dragging it over his head. "Sleeping, or I was. What's the problem, Kendra?"

She paused, and he steeled himself for whatever bad news she was about to fling at him. "I didn't want to do this over the phone, but I couldn't find you yesterday. I wanted to tell you personally that I'm handing in my resignation."

Declan waited for a stone of cold anger to hit, as per usual when he talked to his ex, but it was strangely absent. "Okay. Do you want to talk severance packages? Jon will be in touch once I have it in writing."

He could almost hear her choking on the other end of the phone. "That's it? You don't want to talk me out of it?"

He sat heavily in the armchair by the windows, opening the curtains a crack. It was blindingly bright out. "Not really. I did the best for you that I could, after our breakup. But you had to make a dog's breakfast of the job here in Melbourne. That was not only cruel, it was unprofessional. And I think you know it. I'll be cleaning up after you for months. Tell me when you want to finish up."

"Effective immediately. I have another job starting in the new year."

Declan shrugged. "Fine. Email me your letter of resignation and Jon will sort out the details."

"But Declan, don't you want to know where I'm going?" The whine in her voice was grating on his nerves.

"Not really, no." He ended the call. Maybe it was juvenile to cut her off like that, but he was so done with her.

He stared at his phone for a second, then spotted the actual time. Eleven fifteen. He turned to the bed, to see the gorgeous girl with her jet black hair fanned put on the pillow, her delicate curves covered only by a sheet.

He was pretty sure Yuki didn't have to work today, but she was sound asleep in the Executive Suite, upstairs from the very same people she had been trying to dodge last night. She probably wouldn't be happy about still being here with him.

Declan thought about climbing back into bed, but he wouldn't get back to sleep. Not now. So, he headed for the shower. He needed the hot water, his back was a bit sore (for good reasons) and most of all, he needed time to think, before he talked to Yuki.

He didn't want to end things with her. But would a long-distance relationship be something she was open to?

Declan wasn't superstitious, but her crossed his fingers and made a Christmas wish. Hopefully, Yuki would still be his, after they had a chance to talk.

Yuki pretended to be asleep long enough to hear most of the conversation Declan had with his ex. She was resigning, saying goodbye. It didn't sound too warm and fuzzy. Good. Yuki wanted Declan all to herself, no use denying it.

She rolled over when Declan closed the bathroom door, and then she heard the shower running. With a glance at the clock on her side of the bed, she sat bolt upright. After eleven? Nearly lunchtime?

"Oh no! No, no, no..."

Yuki jumped out of bed and scampered to find her clothes. Just her little silver dress and a Santa jacket?

"No!" She couldn't go downstairs looking like that.

She groaned with frustration as she put on her underwear and dress, baulking at the Santa gear. Imagine if she waltzed past her co-workers dressed like that. They would think she was delusional. If the shift manager saw her, she'd be out on her ear.

Melanie. She could help Yuki out of this mess. Maybe?

Yuki crossed the room to where her handbag lay on the

table next to Declan's wallet. Fishing out her phone, she went to text Mel. She already had a message:

Melanie: Don't come downstairs. Security video! BTW nice hat Mrs Claus. Declan looks sexy ;)

"Noooo!"

The shower was still running in the bathroom. She flicked her head in that direction. Should she stay and talk to Declan, ask him to help her come up with a solution? He was a good man, but he'd have no idea how to help. No. She had to handle this, somehow.

She wrote a quick note on the hotel's fancy stationery, added her phone number, and searched in the wardrobe for one Declan's business shirts.

Yuki quickly popped on a white shirt over her dress, tied a knot in the front to bring it to mid-thigh length, almost completely covering her shiny dress. She tied her hair in a low ponytail and donned her sunglasses too. She checked her reflection in the mirror on the wardrobe door. With her head down, she was almost incognito. She could be any old guest walking out the front door. Hopefully.

"Right. Let's do this."

She was about to make a dash for it, when the bathroom door opened. A cloud of steam and a damp Declan, dressed only in a towel slung low on his hips, emerged with a sexy swagger in his walk. His trademark grin faded as he checked out her outfit, complete with shoes and sunglasses.

His eyebrows lifted, his brow creased. "Going somewhere?"

Her heart stalled for a moment. She had to explain. She yanked off her sunnies. "Oh Declan. It's the worst! Melanie texted me and said I shouldn't go downstairs and there's security video of me in a Santa hat from last night. I'm soooo fired!"

He grimaced, then moved towards her. "Were you just going to leave, without a word?"

"No. I mean yes, but I wrote you a note." She pointed at the table.

Silently, he walked to the table and grabbed the note, reading it in a few seconds. It was brief, it was true. He read it out loud:

Dear Declan,

Had a fun night! Hope to see you later. Call me if you want.

Yuki.

"You added a smiley face. At least you gave me your number before bailing on me. That's something, I guess." His voice was cold as a shard of ice.

Yuki shook her head. "It's not like that. I loved our night together. Honest. I just need to find a way out of here. That's all I can think about for now."

Declan shrugged. "I guess you're going then. I was going to suggest we have breakfast in bed, but if that's not what you want—"

Yuki's face heated. She did want to stay. But he was making this situation all about him! Couldn't he see she was trapped? "I do want to stay, really, but I can't forget about my job, my life, just to hang out with you for a bit longer! You're the one leaving the country tonight."

He stared at her, boring down into the depths of her soul, or it felt like it. "I thought we had something good going on. There could be more than one night. But I guess I was wrong. Wouldn't be the first time." He turned his back on her, and walked slowly back into the bathroom, shutting the door behind him with a definite bang.

She spoke quietly in the empty room. "Oh, hell in a hand-bag. What have I done?"

Yuki grabbed her things, slunk out of the suite and headed straight down the corridor for the elevator they'd taken last night. If she emerged near the restaurant downstairs, she could cut through the dining room and exit onto the side street, totally bypassing Reception. That was the plan.

By the time she hopped out on the Ground floor, she knew she'd made an obvious mistake. Security cameras. The assistant manager, Mr Ivanov, was waiting for her. Yuki's heart pounded, and it was lucky she was wearing sunglasses because her eyes were watery too. Mr Ivanov wasn't a bad guy, he was generally fair, but he looked extremely disappointed. It cut her deeper than she expected.

His dark brown eyes narrowed, exaggerating the crow's feet pattern of lines on his tanned face. Mr Ivanov squinted at her appearance. "Ms Yamimoto. Would you please accompany me to my office?"

She simply nodded and followed him, dragging her feet as if she was a condemned prisoner walking to her own execution.

On the way past Reception, she blinked as Carlos shot her a sympathetic smile, and mouthed the words, *Call me*.

Declan didn't really expect her to be there when he'd got himself under control, brushed off the stupid dampness on his cheeks, and came out of the bathroom. He'd hoped she'd be there, maybe waiting for him back in bed. But that was fantasy stuff, not real life.

Real life was being left, again, by a girl he liked a lot more than was sensible. He huffed out a deep breath and sat down on the edge of the bed in the silent room.

Yuki was a dream girl, not part of his everyday grind. He'd pack his suitcase, get ready to fly home, spend Christmas with his family, get back to work and forget all about her. Except he wouldn't forget about her, because he knew he was lying to himself.

He clenched his fists, then got up, got dressed, dragging

on his jeans and a business shirt. He had to make a couple of calls. The world didn't stop because his heart was beaten up and bruised purple, again.

Declan had to speak to Jon about the whole Kendra thing. He had to decide on the best course of action, and suddenly one option appeared in his mind like the proverbial pot of gold at the end of the rainbow. Maybe he was a sucker, chasing something that didn't exist. But he had to try to fix things, both the business-related mess in the Melbourne office and the personal mess with Yuki.

He made the call. He'd take a chance. He crossed his fingers for luck.

⣀⣀⣀

Yuki didn't usually cry at work, but today was a special occasion. She had never been fired before. She'd nodded along with Mr Ivanov's account of what happened the night before. Yes, she had dated a hotel guest. Yes, that was her entering the hotel at three o'clock in the morning, wearing a Santa hat. Yes, she had spent the night with a guest in his hotel suite.

She didn't want to say anymore, but one phrase slipped out, "I really like him. I didn't want to cause any trouble, but I just really...like him." It sounded pathetic, but it was true.

Mr Ivanov nodded, sighed in an exhausted way, and patted her on the hand. He passed her a box of Kleenex before he left his office, to organise her termination papers and final pay cheque. No Christmas bonus, of course.

Yuki blew her nose into a tissue, and then grabbed her phone from her bag. She messaged Melanie.

Yuki: I'M FIRED. I knew it, but it still sucks. I hope we can still be friends.

Melanie replied immediately.

Melanie: Yes it sucks! Of course we're still friends you big dork! Come see me before you leave, if you can. X

At least she still had one friend among her co-workers. The image of Carlos popped into her head. She texted him too.

Yuki: I'm fired. Happy to hang out sometime though if you still want to keep in touch.

Carlos: Yes! Come to dinner with me and Zack in the new year.

Yuki smiled, and blew her nose again. Carlos and his boyfriend Zack were both lovely guys. And Zack was a chef, so his choice of dinner was bound to be awesome.

Carlos: But first...do you want to leave a note at Reception for your favourite guest?

Yuki froze, staring at her phone. She could do that, send a goodbye note to Declan. No one except Carlos would need to know. But she didn't think she could stroll up to Reception on her way out of the hotel. No, she would leave a note with Melanie and ask her to pass it on.

Yuki: Thanks, you're a gem. I'll be in touch.

She smiled, then sucked in a breath, slapping a hand over her mouth. She had an idea. If the universe truly hated her, it wouldn't work. But if there was a glimmer of hope, something called fate or whatever, she had to try.

The thing she had with Declan could be special, she knew it in her bones. So, she planned out what she would write, everything she'd do, to make sure he knew exactly how she felt. Before he left for Ireland.

Her phone pinged again with another message. No, it was an email. The email she had been waiting for, finally. With trembling fingers, she opened it and read it super quick, then read over it again, making sure of the details.

She squealed so loud she was certain Mr Ivanov would think she'd completely lost her mind. Maybe she had, but in a good way. Only time would tell...

Chapter Seven

Palladian Hotel
Two P.M. on Christmas Eve

Declan headed to Reception to check out, and to order a taxi headed to the airport. Sure, he would be a few hours early for his flight, but he could hang out in the Business Class lounge and get some work done. He wanted nothing more than to get the hell out of the hotel, ASAP.

He wheeled his suitcase behind him as he approached the Reception desk, looking about from side to side, warily. Hopefully the hotel manager wasn't about to accost him and yell at him for corrupting one of his staff.

Declan wouldn't have entirely blamed him. Yuki was younger than him, and she'd been at work when they met. She had warned him when they headed back to the hotel, said it wasn't allowed, but did that stop Declan? Nope. He'd been under the influence of lust, pure and simple. It wasn't like him, at all. Usually, he was in complete control. Cold as a robot, according to Kendra.

When he stood in front of the desk, he half expected Yuki to pop out of the back office and banter with him. But it was a young man, Carlos, her friend maybe, who asked if he could help with anything.

"Wait just one moment, sir." He made a quick phone call, and Declan waited. "Our Events Manager will be down in a moment. She has a matter to discuss with you, if you'd be kind enough to wait."

Declan stared blankly at Carlos. What was this about? Then he remembered: the mezzanine, a snow machine, Yuki spinning around in the pretty white flakes, Santa on a throne being yelled at by her friend with curly hair. Melanie, the Events Manager.

"Yes, sure." Declan stepped to one side, wheeling his suit-case to a spot against a wall, in front of a mini Christmas tree. Carlos nodded, then shot him a wide smile.

Melanie arrived on the scene, her curls bouncing as she speed-walked towards him. "Mr Moriarty, it's a pleasure to meet you." She extended her right hand and he shook it, not sure what was happening. Melanie grinned, placing a large envelope in his other hand.

"I do hope you'll read this over this proposal, Mr Moriarty. The Events Team and many of the staff will be sorry to see you leave before we have had a chance to discuss certain future events. I'm sure you, um, your company, will keep us in mind. For the future."

Very cryptic.

He nodded, and Melanie took his hand again. "Good. I'll be around until seven tonight, if you need anything. Anything at all." She turned and walked away.

He stared after her, then glanced at the envelope in his hand, marked only with his name. Opening it, he laughed as a pile of gold glitter tumbled out. He had a feeling now, this letter could only be from Yuki. He unfolded the paper, read it, careful not to get too much glitter on his shirt.

To Declan,

I'm so sorry I'm not telling you this in person, but I couldn't let you leave the country without telling you how I feel. I'm mad about you. That's basically it. But I want to tell you the whole story.

From the first second I saw you, looking all handsome, I thought I'd love to go out with you. Well, to be honest I thought I'd like to kiss the big white smile right off your face. Then you spoke to me (I was sitting under the Christmas tree, do you remember?) and you had an Irish accent and Oh My God, I nearly swallowed my tongue. I adore an Irish accent, did you know that? You were my idea of perfect. But I never thought you'd really like me.

Anyway, we haven't had nearly enough time to get to know each other, but I wanted to tell you that last night was the BEST night of my life, even if I did get fired. It was totally worth it! Even now, thinking about how you touched me...my face is on fire. Other parts of me too. The fun parts, if you know what I mean?

I want you to know, I like you, a lot. So much, I feel like my heart is going to explode, like a letter full of glitter. Is that a weird thing to say? I don't care. I think I've fallen in love with you, even though I've only known you a few days and that's probably ridiculous. Sometimes I jump into things headfirst without thinking things through...you might have noticed!

Please don't leave without saying goodbye, properly. If I haven't burnt my bridges or traumatised you with glitter, I'd like to invite you to my apartment to talk. We can have dinner if you want to. I want you to come over. Just in case I wasn't clear, again.

My address in Elwood is below.

Lots of love (and kisses),

Yuki xxx

P.S. When you were dressed up as Santa and you kissed me, that was totally a fantasy of mine. That was probably a weird thing to tell you too. But I'm glad I did.

Declan folded the letter and chuckled under his breath. Yuki was some girl. She could still be *his* girl, if he played his cards right.

He wandered back to the Reception desk in a haze of conflicting emotions. He wanted her, yes. But he had to make her understand, he was a busy man. His life wasn't all neatly wrapped up in a box marked 'boyfriend material'. He wouldn't be around all the time. She might not want him if she understood all that. But then again, she might.

He glanced up to find Carlos watching him, his eyes sparkling. Declan stuffed the letter in his back pocket.

"Do you want me to order you a taxi to the airport, sir? Or somewhere else if you prefer?" Carlos was obviously a friend of Yuki's too. Good to know.

Declan smiled, he couldn't help it. "Elwood, thanks. I have to see a friend before I fly out."

The joy on Carlos's face was clear as day. "Excellent, sir."

Yuki's apartment
Elwood, Melbourne

Yuki dashed around her apartment like a busy bee in springtime, tidying up already tidy tables and her spotless little kitchen. She was dressed in her pink underwear and a giant Hard Candy band shirt, with a picture of a shattered candy cane. Perfect for Christmas.

Her flatmate Claudia was already gone for Christmas break, having headed to the country to stay with her family. So, she had the place all to herself, luckily. Declan might be coming over, hopefully, if he'd read her letter. If he still liked her. If her wish came true. She wanted everything to be ready.

She danced along to the radio, into her bedroom. She straightened the silver quilt on her bed, fluffed the pillows and lit a few vanilla scented candles on the side tables. There.

Everything was pretty and ready. Her stomach rolled over. *She* wasn't ready!

She sprinted to her wardrobe and scanned her options. Little red dress? Super festive, but maybe too much with all the sequins? Blue spaghetti strap sundress? Cute-sexy. That was a winner. She was about to get changed when the apartment's door buzzer went off.

She checked her reflection in the bedroom mirror. "Um, you'll have to do. You're super cute, Yuki. Any man would be lucky to have you." She breathed out slowly.

She didn't quite believe the affirmations that Melanie suggested she practice, but maybe they helped her confidence, a little.

She made her way to the front door, answering the intercom. "Who is it?"

"Declan." His voice was extra deep. Sexy. She bit her lip.

"Please, come upstairs." She danced on the spot while she waited, trying to get rid of her nerves. He knocked a few moments later, and she unlocked the door, flinging it wide open.

He was beautiful. A lock of hair flopped over his forehead, and his blue shirt matched the shade of his eyes. The force of him struck her again, like some kind of mystical lightning. He leaned on his suitcase, and she wished he was staying with her.

"Declan." Yuki grinned, her heart hammering as she stepped back to let him inside. "Thank you so much for coming over. My flatmate is a guerrilla knitter, be warned. She's gone away for a few days." She extended her arm to show him in and closed the door behind him.

He was close enough to smell the scent of his aftershave. She wanted to kiss his gorgeous face. Take him straight to the bedroom. But he brushed past her, without meeting her eyes. She didn't want it to go this way, all cold and formal.

Now Declan tipped his head to one side, and she felt his

eyes on her, running up and down the length of her body. His face was serious though. "Should I ask what on earth a guerrilla knitter is?"

"Come through to the lounge room, you'll see."

Declan left his suitcase near the front door, glanced around the apartment and he soon figured out the guerrilla knitter thing. Lamps were wrapped in multi-coloured knitted cosies, knitted wall hangings decorated every spare inch of space, even a knitted plant holder sat on the coffee table, a wilting fern almost hidden inside it. A small silver Christmas tree sat on the kitchen counter, covered in knitted decorations. Guerrilla knitting, indeed.

Yuki ushered him over to a big blue sofa, and he followed her, watching as the fabric of the t-shirt she wore swayed when she walked. It barely covered her round little bottom. He swallowed, hard.

He sat on one end of the sofa, and he thought she'd stick to the other end. But she sat only a couple of inches away. Her bare thighs taunted him, daring him to touch.

He cleared his throat. "I got your letter." He held up his palm, so she could see the sparkles clinging to his skin. He was ridiculously nervous, and his hand shook.

She laughed, and pressed her hand to his, threaded their fingers together. He let out a long breath.

"Yuki, I—"

"Declan, I meant—"

He laughed, and she did too. The ice was broken.

"You go first," he said, watching her face go soft, a gentle expression of...love? Caring, at least.

She let her words come out in a great rush. "I meant to tell you how much I already care about you. But then, I thought I was going to lose my job, and I panicked. It was all too much, all at once. I really wanted to spend more time with you."

Declan lifted her hand to his mouth and kissed the back of her hand, and something inside him relaxed when he heard her sigh. "Did you actually lose your job? Because I'd feel terrible about that."

She let a quasi-smile cross her face, one dimple creasing her cheek. "Yes. But it's okay now. I didn't get a chance to tell you, I interviewed for another job a few weeks ago. Actually, it was three interviews, and I thought I must be on the short-list. I got it! I just found out this afternoon."

He watched her eyes, lit up with excitement. "That's grand. Tell me about it." He half listened to her answer, all the while watching her lips.

"I'm going to be a flight attendant with Mermaid Airlines! You know, the funnest airline in the world. It's so exciting because I've always wanted to travel, but I haven't been anywhere except here, and Japan and Singapore with my family when I was a kid. So anyway, I have to fly out in a few days for training, in London!"

"London? But I thought...I thought you'd be living here." He held his breath, waiting for what she'd say next.

Yuki pushed her loose hair back behind her ear. "It's only for a couple of weeks. They want me back in Melbourne as my home base, as well as flying to lots of cool places. But I'd love to move to London one day."

Declan's heart had swelled in his chest, but it relaxed again until he could breathe properly. "That's grand. I mean, fantastic. I organised some work stuff too, rearranged things so I could be here for a few months. In Melbourne."

Her mouth popped open, and he wanted to kiss her, right that second. "You did? Why, Declan?"

No use beating around the bush now. "Partly for work-related reasons. Someone who knows the business needs to take the reins in the Asia Pacific office, so it might as well be me. But mostly, for you, Miss Yuki. I wanted to stay here, to see more of you. To take you out, to stay in with you. To kiss you. A lot."

Her smile grew from something fragile, to a full bloom across her pretty face. "Oh. In that case…" She shuffled across until she sat on his lap. "Merry Christmas to me."

"Merry Christmas to me, too."

Then he kissed her delicious lips. He kept right on kissing her until they were both short of breath. God, he couldn't get enough of her. The way she was squirming on his lap told him she felt the same way.

He palmed her firm bottom, squeezing her flesh through the soft shirt she wore like a dress. Heat and the promise of pleasure thundered through his whole body.

Yuki pulled away from their kiss and touched his cheek. "Come with me."

Yuki took Declan's hand, the one still covered in glitter, and led him straight to her bedroom.

He was mostly quiet, but when he entered the room fully, he whispered, "I've been dying to see your bedroom."

"Really? It's not that fancy."

Declan looked around the room and said, "It's totally you. Those little stars on the ceiling, the silver curtains, the pink armchair, the quotes and postcards on the wall. All of it."

He faced her again, pulling her into a hug, close to his body. She rested her head on his broad chest. "Sweet, pretty, full of fun and dreams."

She shrugged, but heat flooded her face. "Huh. You like it, then?"

He spoke low in her ear. "I love it. Adore it, really." He kissed the base of her throat.

Oh, hello heart explosion! She didn't have it in her to play it cool, when he was being so adorable himself.

She lifted her head, meeting his eyes. "Get in my bed. What are you waiting for?"

He laughed, low and rumbly. "Such a polite invitation."

Okay, maybe she did need to cool it, a bit. But he moved towards the bed and started removing his clothes, so that was the important thing. First his shirt went, tossed on her pink chair, revealing acres of lovely man-skin.

Then he unbuttoned the fly of his jeans and she had to press a hand to her mouth. He was...bigger, in the daylight. Of course, she remembered the feel of him, the pressure inside her when they came together, everything just right. Now everything low in her abdomen tightened, in memory, in anticipation.

His shoes and jeans were gone in a moment, and his grey boxer briefs were stupidly sexy, in that unassuming guy way. He probably didn't even know he had that poet-slash-rockstar thing going on, the way he flexed his bicep with his interesting tattoo. He looked at her from under a lock of his thick wavy hair.

Yuki let out a long, shaky breath. She still had far too many clothes on. So, she jumped up on her bed, dragged her shirt up over her head and tossed it away. She shook out her hair, hoping she looked nicely rumpled and not like a hot mess. When she raised her eyes again, Declan was standing there like a statue, still halfway across the room. His eyes were on her, the smoulder of his stare burning her up from the inside out.

"God, Yuki. Look at you." He stalked over to the bed, climbing up to meet her, pushing her down gently so she rested on her pillows. "So beautiful."

Declan must have liked her hot pink lace underwear. His

hands were all over her knickers, and then, *oh yes*, inside them. He kissed her lips, slowly, pressing kisses to the corners of her mouth, then down her throat again, making her want... more. She gasped when he made his way down to her breasts, kissing her right through the fabric of her skimpy bra.

"Declan," she breathed, "I want you now. I want to ride you."

"Grrrrmph." He bit down on her nipple, making her full-on squeal.

He rolled off her, eyes wide, lips wet from kissing, looking completely wild. "Condom?"

"I bought a whole lot of them. See?" She pulled open the drawer of her bedside table. Piles of colourful condoms spilled out.

Declan raised an arched eyebrow. "Now I'm going to have performance anxiety."

She bit her lip. "Oh, no pressure, I only wanted to be prepared. And I liked the colours."

He grinned, showing lots of teeth. "Joking! I was messing with you." Grabbing a condom, a nice royal blue, he sat on the edge of the bed and got rid of his underwear. He prepared to sheath himself, but Yuki wanted to touch him.

"Let me." She shuffled over to him, to sit on her knees beside him. "God, you're built. I mean, I love your body, Declan."

He groaned, handing over the condom. She took her time, running her hand over the hard length of him, circling him, squeezing just a little...

"Yuki, please." His voice cracked on her name. *Oooh*, she liked that. Who was begging now?

In a second she sheathed him, and then she peeled off her remaining scraps of clothes. Totally naked, she straddled him, wrapping her legs around his strong back. His eyes were on her, on every inch of her. She shivered.

When she first raised herself up, then sank down on him,

he filled her so completely, she could hardly breathe. Declan's face was pressed to her neck, and the sound he made nearly brought on her climax. So gruff, so deep.

She shifted, rising and falling, rocking her hips. Yuki pressed herself down, hard, and found her rhythm. Declan rose beneath her too, giving her what she needed, angling his hips. He kissed her deeply, tasting her, pressing his body to hers, until she was undone. Her heart throbbed as the heat inside her unfurled, spread, took her over. She threw back her head, cried out, and chased the stars.

Declan held her, a firm hand on her waist. Grinding himself against her, thrusting again and again. He called her name when he fell back, limp and spent. And she lay on top of him, smoothing her hand over his chest, caressing him, so glad to have found him.

So happy to love him.

"Yuki? Are you awake?" Declan whispered the words by Yuki's cheek. She was lying beside him, her head on her pillow, eyes closed, beautiful as an angel.

"Mmmm. Maybe."

He chuckled, stroking her cheek with his thumb. "Hey Miss Yuki, I'll have to leave soon."

She sat up suddenly, the sheets dropping away from her perfect breasts. "What? Not already?" She brushed a strand of her hair out of her face.

He couldn't help stroking her hair, then stroking her breast. "It's nearly nine o'clock. My flight's at quarter to midnight, but I'll have to get a move on."

She dropped back down to lie next to him, and kissed him, and his heart could hardly take it. He didn't want to go.

He'd never wanted to stay with someone more, than with her, at that moment.

"Stay, a bit longer. Have some dessert."

They had already had dinner, in bed, home delivery from some restaurant where she knew the chef. "I think I had my dessert, even seconds. You were delicious."

"Mmmm."

He sighed, placing his hand on her waist. "What are you doing for Christmas? You haven't told me."

She glanced up at him, her eyes dancing. "I'm having lunch with my parents, and my brother's back home from Singapore. Maybe my aunts and cousins will be there. We'll eat a turkey, and sushi, and Pavlova, then play a ruthless game of Monopoly. It should be fun."

Declan squeezed her waist, let his hand wander lower to her hip. "It sounds like fun. I wish I was staying."

Yuki pressed a kiss on his cheek. "You know, I think you're the first man I'd like to bring home, to meet my family."

His chest felt too tight. She was so sweet. He felt the same, knew his parents would absolutely love her. "Not Glenn the Arsehole Ex?"

She rolled her eyes. "Urgh. He said he thought it was cool I'm Japanese, well, my family is. He wanted to collect girl-friends from the world. As if we were commemorative plates and he needed the complete set."

He sat up, crossing his arms. "Right, do you need me to hunt him down?"

She shook her head. "No, I want you to come back and see me soon, not have to find bail money."

He nodded. "Fair point." He kissed her forehead, then her lips. "I will be back soon, you know. We can do this, have dessert, whatever you want."

Yuki smiled, her cheeks rosy and warm when he touched her there. "Oh, you'd better be back soon. I can hardly wait."

She leaned over and grabbed another little coloured

packet from the bedside table. "Here, you'd better give me something else to dream about." She waved the packet in his face, as he flipped her over and growled in her ear.

"Yes, Miss Yuki. Anything you want."

Mermaid Airlines Head Office, London, UK
Two weeks later...

Yuki did her best to shimmy in time to the music along with the other airline recruits, but her belly was full of ninja-fighting butterflies and she felt like an uncoordinated loser. Who knew you had to learn a weird dance to be a Mermaid Airlines flight attendant? Apparently, everyone else who went for the job already knew. And they could dance.

Falling off her high heels as she did a twist to her right, Yuki slammed right into the pretty blonde girl in full uniform, standing behind her. She'd got her right in the stomach.

"Ooof, I'm so sorry!"

The Trainer at the front of the room shook her head, then threw her hands in the air. "Cut the music. Let's take a ten minute break."

The other girl had fallen, sprawling on her side on the polished wooden floors. Yuki dropped into a crouch beside her. "I'm sorry, again. Here, let me help you up."

The girl looked up, her blonde ponytail swinging behind her. "Thank you. I'm grand though, really. No harm done."

Yuki stared at her. "You're Irish! Do you know how much I love an Irish accent? I think we're going to be great friends."

The injured girl giggled, sitting up straight. "If you say so. I'm Sinead. Good to meet you." Sinead took Yuki's hand, and scrambled to her feet. Then she smoothed down her uniform and straightened up to show off perfect posture.

"I'm Yuki. It's good to meet you too, Sinead." Yuki tipped

her head to one side, studying Sinead. She seemed to be full of confidence. "Have you been with the airline for a while?"

Sinead nodded, her pale blue eyes striking. "A few years. I said I'd help train some of you new recruits. Be a mentor if you like."

Yuki straightened her own dress, not as elegant as the proper uniform. She couldn't wait to try it on. But who knew if she'd even pass the exams? She dropped her voice so the other trainees didn't overhear her. "I'd love for you to be my mentor. I think I'll need the help."

Sinead smiled, and she looked genuinely kind. "Do you want to grab a coffee with me? We can have a chat. The café downstairs is pretty good."

Yuki nodded and followed Sinead towards the training room door. Sinead seemed like someone who would be a good friend. Yuki may not know much about emergency procedures or how to make sure the overhead compartments were secure, not yet. But she knew people, and often had a sense of what they were thinking. Working in the hotel had taught her that at least.

Yuki's phone buzzed in her jacket pocket, as they headed into the corridor. "Oh, I wonder who could be texting me." She grabbed her phone and read the message. It was Declan.

Declan: I'm heading to London for a few days. Be there Friday. :)

She was no doubt grinning like a kid on Christmas morning, because Sinead asked, "Was that your boyfriend?"

She shrugged, playing it cool. "It's very new, but I really like him."

Sinead's lips tipped up at the corners, then she sighed. "Good for you. I should be so lucky."

Yuki stopped walking to read Declan's next message.

Declan: Miss you, Miss Yuki.

She replied, before she got too excited thinking about the

weekend coming up. She wouldn't be able to concentrate if she let her imagination run wild.

Yuki: Miss you too. Bring me a present from Ireland! Pretty please?

Declan: Since you asked so nicely, pretty girl. Call you later.

Yuki: xxx

Sinead spoke, as they started walking again. "Are you still up for coffee?"

Yuki nodded. "Yes. I'm up for anything."

As she walked, Yuki's mind whirled. Maybe the thing between her and Declan would work out, even with them both working and travelling all the time. She hoped so.

She pressed her fingertips to the stunning necklace Declan had hidden under her tiny Christmas tree, before he left for Dublin. It was a swirly silver heart, from Tiffany's. She loved it. She hoped he liked the deluxe Santa hat and red silk tie she had couriered to his parents' house.

The new year was turning out to be an amazing ride so far. Her life of adventure had officially begun. Hopefully soon she'd be travelling the world, having adventures she'd couldn't even imagine yet.

Sinead winked at her, as she showed Yuki into the elevator, pretending to demonstrate the way to the emergency exits. "Let's go, Mermaid crew."

Mermaid crew. Yuki liked the sound of that. A lot.

Girl on a Babymoon

A Girl on a Plane Novelette

Cassandra O'Leary

Author's Note

ON GIRL ON A BABYMOON

Dear reader,

I wrote this novelette in 2022 based on an idea I had a couple of years ago to revisit Sinead and Gabriel, the lead characters from my debut novel, *Girl on a Plane*. Please note, the events in this story take place five years after the events in that book, around the time of the couple's fifth anniversary. I hope that's not a spoiler!

I recommend you read *Girl on a Plane* first, if you haven't already. You should still be able to understand the story as a stand alone though, but please be aware the characters are a long-term couple by this stage.

Cheers,

Cassandra x

Chapter One

Melbourne, Australia

Sinead had no hope of containing her giggles as she stared at her phone's screen, but she slapped a hand over her mouth anyway. She half snorted, half coughed into her palm before shaking her head to get herself under control. The Uber driver would think she'd lost her mind, but who cared about that? Not today, she didn't.

She clicked out of the amazing image on her phone screen and stared out the car's passenger side window instead, watching the streetscape whiz by in a blur of colours, sky blue, white and grey. The warm fuzzies in her belly settled, fluttered and subsided.

Gabriel was going to absolutely love her anniversary surprise. Love. Adore. Worship at her feet and hopefully worship every last nook and curve of her whole body in minute, sensual detail. Several times. *Oh, yes.* This anniversary trip had been an excellent idea. How could they have been married for five years already?

She didn't know how her news would go down with Gabriel. Hopefully, he'd be on board. All she had to do was let him know what she wanted and fill him in on the plan. She sighed, exhausted suddenly. He would be pleased, wouldn't he? Happy? It was a lot to take in. She'd had a minor freak out already.

He'd be okay, she was almost positive. He'd research this like he would with a business deal or an investment. He was good at details, her Gabriel. The best at everything he did. Having a man like him, so focused and determined in everything, work and play, had turned out very nicely in their relationship so far, especially in the bedroom. The only problem was, sometimes he was a wee bit put off by spontaneous changes of plan.

He'd love her surprise. And if he didn't bloody love it, she was possibly going to have him killed. Or at least torture him in a sexy way until he admitted he loved her and her surprise, and then he could do the minute detail worshipping of her body.

Yes, that was a plan. She grinned and rubbed her hands together with pure, undiluted, only slightly evil glee.

She gave a nod and word of thanks to the Uber driver, a very sweet man named Aziz who often drove her home from work at the luxury travel agency she ran at Gabriel's office building in the city. She straightened out her shirt and threw her phone in her bag. The car rolled to a stop.

In one mostly elegant motion, she launched herself and her handbag out of the car and onto the footpath, then she was clacking along in her electric blue high heels. Her phone was in her hand, tapping on her husband's name and he answered the call before she'd even taken five steps towards the front door of their beachfront townhouse.

"Hello, Irish." His voice was gravelly and rumbly, pinging her pleasure centre and tugging at something in her abdomen. She bit her lower lip and almost tripped over the spiky plant near her front steps.

Sinead pressed her lips together before the exciting words exploded out of her in a great rush.

Control. Plan the announcement. Don't freak him out.

Sinead nearly peed herself from the effort of keeping it inside. She released her lower lip and took a shuddery breath. "Ah, it's the man himself. Are you looking especially handsome on this fine day? I'll bet you are."

"I was just thinking about you."

She grinned so hard her cheeks ached. "All good thoughts, I hope. Maybe naked thoughts?"

He chuckled, deep and low in her ear. "Always good, and many naked thoughts of you, my love."

She sighed, leaning her right side against the front door as she fumbled for her keys in the depths of her bag. "I just got home. I hope you're ready for some news. But I can't tell you right now, because we have to get ready to go."

There was a slight pause from Gabriel. "Go? Ah, is there somewhere I've forgotten I should be right now?"

The trepidation in her husband's voice gave her pause. Sinead knew of Gabriel's one o'clock appointment with Dyer and Sons, the eco builders who would hopefully be working on their upcoming island resort project. She didn't want to disrupt that meeting or their plans for a fabulous new business venture, but she'd definitely do just that if she hit Gabriel with her news over the phone.

"No, you're good. I meant, we have to leave by five this afternoon for our surprise weekend getaway. Before you say anything else, it's a *surprise*, so that's why you didn't know about it."

She unlocked the front door, kicked off her shoes and crossed the living room, a welcoming open plan space dominated by a long sage green plush sofa that made her want to throw herself right on it and lie down. So, she did. She lay flat on her back, her head on the overstuffed silver cushion at one end, phone pressed to her ear.

Gabriel's deep chuckle resonated in her ear, and somewhere deep in her belly. "Oh, is this one of those surprises where I'm going to suddenly find myself naked, tied to a chair and unable to move for days? Because if that's the case, go ahead and pack my bag for me."

The giggles rose from Sinead's belly and escaped her lips with a kind of squeak. "Will do, husband mine."

"Just let me get this meeting out of the way, then I'm all yours for the weekend."

All mine. Yes.

"Stay at the office and I'll pick you up at quarter to five. Okay?"

"Anything you wish, Irish."

Sinead closed her eyes, counting every single one of her blessings. There were quite a lot these days. "Love you."

"Love you more. Bye." Gabriel signed off, competitive to the last.

Sinead smiled, her cheek muscles stretching out as she ended the call. She'd have to hurry to get everything organised. But first, maybe she'd have a little rest.

She popped her phone on the coffee table and settled in for a power nap.

"Oh my God!" Sinead woke with a start, jumping up to a sitting position on her sofa. How long had she been asleep?

A buzzing noise, then a sing-song tune came from somewhere nearby. Her phone.

She slapped a hand to her forehead. Her head was muzzy, clouded with the tail-ends of her dream, of herself and Gabriel holed up in their island paradise getaway. It was warm, deliciously naughty. . .

She looked about the room, reorienting herself and sadly shaking off the remnants of dream-world Gabriel's touch. She grabbed her phone from the coffee table.

Damn! Three missed calls. It was already after five o'clock! She had to meet Gabriel at his office.

She was on her feet and ready to race to the door, when her head started spinning. She flopped back down on the sofa and waited it out. She could leave in a minute, she wouldn't be horribly late.

Wait, she still had to pack their bags. *Oh, no.* Now they would be late for their flight. A click echoed in the quiet house, and Sinead wrenched her neck to the side to find the front door had swung open. Gabriel was framed in the door-way. He was home!

"Sinead, my God. Can you answer your damn phone?" He stormed towards her, emanating waves of tension.

He stood in front of her, running a hand through his already tousled blonde hair so it stuck up in front. Adorable. "Are you alright? Bloody hell, you had me worried when you didn't show up."

She shook her head. She'd never meant to get him so worried. "Sorry, I fell asleep. It was the strangest thing—" She shut her mouth with a snap of her jaw. "I haven't been feeling one hundred percent. I guess I needed the rest."

All the air apparently whooshed out of Gabriel's mouth in a huge sigh laden with relief. Or more worry? "You'd tell me if there was something wrong, wouldn't you?"

He sat beside her, carefully taking her hand in his. The warmth of his touch was a balm to her very soul, as always. The slightly rough texture of his palm rasped over her smooth skin, making her want him, his hands on her body, as always. He'd always be hers, she knew it. But still she hesitated to spill her news without warning.

"I saw my doctor this morning. She said I need to make sure I get enough rest, concentrate on eating healthy. Not too much stress." So far, so true. She had to look after herself, now more than ever.

Gabriel reached over and smoothed his hand through her loose hair, smoothing a lock behind her ear. "Is it work? Opening the new agency has been demanding. I feel like I've hardly seen you for weeks."

That was true, too. Sinead had been burning the candle at both ends, until she'd basically burned her own butt off. She'd only just finished her final semester of her business and tourism degree, now a new business was taking all her time and energy. That would have to change.

"I'll slow down, I promise. Now, I really do want to take you away for the weekend. I need some alone time with my handsome husband. But I think we've missed our flight." She bit the inside of her lip. Why did she have to ruin their getaway?

Gabriel nodded once, his sky blue eyes shining as he turned her chin towards him with the tip of his finger. "Let's take the jet."

Well, she'd always thought he was perfect. Imagine, going from a nearly cancelled weekend away one minute, to flying on a private jet the next! Her lips stretched out in a wide smile. "What an excellent idea."

Gabriel's own lips kicked up at one corner. "You know what else is an excellent idea? Kissing you. Right now."

Her stomach flipped, and not with nausea she'd been battling for the past two weeks. She shuffled closer to Gabriel until she was leaning against his shoulder. He swept her hair back into his fist and turned her head until she was pliant and ready under his grasp. She'd become nothing but jelly. The delicious kind, possibly raspberry flavour.

When their lips pressed together, softly at first, she let out a sigh. When she lightly bit his lower lip, Gabriel's moan emanated from somewhere deep inside his body. Their tongues tangled and she found herself sitting on his lap, then his hand gripped her hip through her little stretchy dress. The heat of him, the scent of him, like the ocean mixed with something light and citrusy, made her want to eat him up.

Their lips pressed together hard, Gabriel's touch demanding more. Then he pulled away, his gaze meeting hers in such a way. . . a question in his expression.

She answered him with a brief shake of her head, but she couldn't help squeezing his deliciously firm bicep at the same time. He looked as if he was about to throw her over his shoulder and drag her off to their bedroom, caveman style.

"Not yet, Mr Impatient. Let's get to our super fancy hotel room for our weekend away first. I want you to be absolutely dying to touch me."

The sound he made this time was a growl of frustration, smothered when he kissed her neck. Heat spread over every inch of her skin, making her gasp.

When he pulled away, his familiar half-smile on his face, Gabriel muttered something suspiciously like *"going to make you scream"*.

Sinead couldn't sit still. Her whole body was a-tingle just thinking about it. Not too long to wait . . .

Chapter Two

The private jet base was a space of such luxury, past-Gabriel could have barely imagined it existed. They pulled up in the town car outside the hangar-style building, engineered in such a way that a giant swoop of reflective metal seemed to curve up to the sky, and hang in mid-air above the entrance.

It was an exclusive space, and a doorway to an invitation-only world. As a kid of a single mother, an amazing woman who'd done everything she could to provide for him and bring him up on her own, he'd never understood they were poor. Not until he'd started high school on a scholarship. Then he realised his second-hand clothes and his mum's beaten-up Toyota marked him as different, lesser, at his exclusive private school.

The kid he'd been back then had vowed that one day, things would be different. He'd look after his mother, and he'd have the kind of money that meant she'd never want for anything. And he had looked after her, even when she'd been so ill with early-onset Alzheimer's over the past few years. Even when she'd failed to remember him.

Now that she'd passed away, now that the worst of his grief had passed, he could spend his money spoiling his beautiful wife, and on his growing business of course. Plus, he wanted to do some good in the world.

Gabriel would never have thought of investing in a jet exclusively for their company, until his partner, Ryan, had explained how much easier it would be to travel to remote islands for their new eco resort business. Also, it was *cool*. Big boys and their toys and all that. So, here they were.

He ducked his head as he emerged from their limo, where they'd pulled up under the sweeping roofline of the jet base entrance.

He and Sinead were ready and waiting to fly off to *somewhere*. She'd flat-out refused to tell him where they were headed, and to be fair, if it was a surprise he'd planned, he wouldn't have spilled the beans either. She'd dealt with the ground staff by phone and messaged the pilot, some old friend of hers from her Mermaid Airlines flight attendant days. Apparently, the flight plan was ready.

Sinead was such a natural at organising trips and tours, it was no wonder why she was rocking it in the luxury travel business. She was bright, brilliant and beautiful. He glanced at her, straightening her cute little blue dress while jogging in heels, juggling a phone pressed to one ear. Amazing. And she was his.

She grinned at him, and his heart did that stuttering thing it sometimes did around her. God, he loved her. That was exactly why he'd planned his own surprise for her. Fingers crossed, she'd love his big idea as much as he thought she would.

Sinead chatted as they entered the main building, walking by his side, holding his hand. "This place is so cool. The architecture. All the curved lines. The glass and steel. Wow! It's like the Louvre had a baby with the new aquarium. Oh, but you're going to adore our room on the island too."

He grinned, then turned a sideways glance in her direction. "So, it's an island resort? That's where we're staying?"

Sinead narrowed her eyes at him. "Yes. But no more sneaky hints for you, my love." She reached up and kissed the edge of his jaw.

Just that small touch had him aching for her. And he suspected she knew it. The way she smiled, then bit her full lower lip had him wanting to bite her in return. His wife loved to tease him. He loved it right back, of course.

Sinead tugged on his hand, as a concierge appeared out of nowhere to check their passports and direct them to the dining area. "Right. I think we need some dinner. I hear there's a brilliant menu at this place."

Another staff member in an all-black uniform was scurrying around with their bags, getting them ready to check through to their jet. Gabriel took Sinead's hand in his, and led her through to their table, apparently also reserved in advance. The concierge made sure they were settled and provided with menus.

Gabriel helped Sinead into her seat, taking the opportunity to kiss her temple. She was stunning, his wife. Funny too. Always so thoughtful. He couldn't believe his luck most of the time. People told him he was a lucky bastard, and one look at Sinead proved it was true.

Sinead sighed, tilting her head to one side. Looking him up and down. "So, I might have organised a little something special this weekend for a reason."

He shuffled his leather upholstered chair closer to the white-clothed table, leaning in over a tea-light candle. "Is that so? Can I take a guess?" He was the one teasing now. He had a pretty good idea what was going on.

She raised her gently curved eyebrows, her pale eyes twinkling with mischief. "Ah, this could be fun. Okay, guess away." With a wave of her hand she told him to proceed.

"It's a special occasion, right?" He pressed his hand to his forehead, feigning one of his infamous migraines. That was it. *A migraine.* Not just any old headache. A headache that had literally changed the course of his life.

"It's the anniversary of the weekend when we met, five years ago. When I got chatting to you after our plane was grounded. There was that typhoon and, coincidentally, right after meeting you, I had the mother of all headaches." If he implied she was the source of his migraine, what of it? He could tease her, too.

Sinead's narrowed eyes were the only warning before she stomped on his foot under the table.

"Ow!" He grabbed his foot in one hand, rubbing the sharp pain away. "You'll pay for that, Irish."

She leaned back in her own seat and crossed her arms beneath her breasts. This move never failed to rouse his baser male interest. He could have kissed her. He could have torn her dress off her, right at the table. But a quick glance up at her eyes told him she hadn't quite forgiven his thoughtless comment.

On the other hand, her lips were definitely pouty. Pouty but kissable. He straightened up and mentally talked himself down from hauling her into one of the private bathrooms for a pre-flight quickie.

Not yet. I need her alone. Naked.

She sighed, as if she'd decided to put up with him, but under sufferance. "You were supposed to say something about how you met the most beautiful flight attendant in the world, and you fell in love, irrevocably. Forever. And how I didn't let you get away when you tried to be a noble idiot, saving me from a fate worse than death, in other words, a relationship with you."

"Right. *That.* I knew there was something I'd forgotten. My beautiful Irish goddess. The absolute best thing in my life. Thank you for saving me from a life as a lonely, noble idiot."

Now, Sinead grinned, her gorgeous secret smile. She also

let her little high heeled shoe drop off her foot, and the delicate instep of her bare foot slid up the inside leg of his jeans. He couldn't help staring when her pink tongue licked along her lower lip, in that way she had when she was about to say something ridiculously cheeky. His blood thundered through his veins. That quickie was looking like a real possibility. Until they were rudely interrupted.

Simon, his travel company's concierge, cleared his throat from somewhere to his right. Gabriel shifted in his seat, dragging his attention away from Sinead's mouth with some difficulty.

Simon nodded at them both, then explained what was happening in his no-nonsense way. "Sir, I've been notified that your flight is almost ready to depart. Sorry to delay your dinner, but the chef can provide your meal on board the jet. There's a minor storm predicted en route so we want to stay ahead of it."

"Ah, of course. Lead the way."

Gabriel rose and extended his hand to Sinead. She squeezed his palm, then reached up on his toes so she could whisper in his ear, "A storm coming. Remind you of anything?"

Remind him of anything? Only the best one-night stand of his life. One night that never actually ended. Because the weekend he met Sinead in First Class on a flight that was grounded in Singapore, a storm turned out to be the thing that brought them together. Holed up in a hotel room, touching, kissing. Making his head simultaneously ache and spin with the implications of that old cliché: *love at first sight*. Or, love at first flight, in their case.

He kissed the spot under her left ear that always made her gasp. She responded to his touch like she was on fire, like she couldn't burn without him. Her cheeks flushed pink, her full lips parted. Like she couldn't get enough.

Yes. That. That was what he remembered. What he'd never forget.

Somewhere over the east coast of Australia

Sinead stretched her legs out in front of her, taking turns to rotate her ankles in little circles. The habit was ingrained after years of working as a flight attendant because no-one wanted swollen cankles upon landing in some exotic location.

She'd kicked off her shoes a few minutes after take-off, rubbing her feet on the plush carpet like a contented cat.

She shot a glance at Gabriel, who held her hand on the armrest between them, even as his head lolled to one side. Fast asleep, looking peaceful as an angel.

But he was overworked, her husband. Fine lines bracketed his eyes now, that weren't there five years ago when they first met. Of course, a little age looked good on a handsome man. Refined, mature. *Bastards.*

Women with fair skin like hers often aged like spoiled milk. Who cared about diamonds? Sunscreen was a girl's best friend. And coffee, of course. She sipped her latte and enjoyed the bittersweet taste of it, despite it being decaf.

The sun set outside the jet's window, painting the horizon a luminous shade of orange flecked with bubblegum pink, over a deep navy blue ocean. That kind of view never got old. She leaned forward, until her nose was almost pressed against the glass. *There.* The Whitsunday Islands came into view, a string of havens more exclusive than the finest pearls. Little teardrop shaped gems, surrounded by white sand like encrusted diamonds.

Gabriel squeezed her hand, and her breathing stuttered. How did he cause such a reaction? "Are we almost there? I can't believe I fell asleep," he whispered.

When she turned around so her eyes met his, she blinked

from the impact of his blue eyes, crystal clear and unguarded, as he only was with her. He'd always had the ability to look deep inside her, to know her innermost thoughts. Well, he didn't know all of them this time.

She flashed him a smile. "You bombed out, my angel. Anyway, we're approaching the island now."

Gabriel's lips twisted to one side. "Still no hint as to where we're staying?"

"Aye, here's a hint: there's a view from every room."

"Mmm-hmm. Informative. Practically a guided tour."

Sinead smoothed her ponytail over her shoulder as she carefully chose her next words. "When we get there, we need to talk about something."

The serious note in her voice must have grabbed his attention. He squeezed her hand as he asked, "Are you alright? Sinead, seriously. Tell me."

She nodded, trying not to freak out. Now he probably thought she was dying or something. Which she definitely was not. It was only a major change to their lifestyle, their future plans, level of responsibilities, freedom and of course the physical strain on her. She was trying not to think about that. If it was a hundred years ago, she actually could have died.

Not freaking out, not at all.

"I'm fine. We're fine." Her voice came out as almost a whisper, as their flight attendant approached down the aisle.

She glanced at the younger woman, someone she'd known well enough to say hello to years ago. Blonde hair, perfectly groomed, a little like Sinead herself as a flight attendant starting out. To be fair, this woman was probably more beautiful than Sinead had been. More glossy, somehow. What was her name? Jessica. . . something.

"Hello Jessica, it's grand to see you again." Sinead plastered her fake happy face on, but it had been a while and maybe it didn't stick.

Jessica raised an eyebrow, her eyes darting between herself and Gabriel. "Yes, you too. Your dinner service is ready. Can I offer you a glass of champagne?" She batted her eyelashes. "Mr Anderson? Anything special for you?"

Oooh, that was underhanded. Flirting with a woman's husband right in front of her, regardless of whether she was only a former flight attendant and he was a rich, gorgeous young CEO.

"Thanks Jessica, but I'm perfectly happy." Gabriel leaned in and kissed Sinead's cheek.

Sinead's head spun a little. He was a keeper all right.

Their dinner was served before Gabriel had a chance to say another word. In their proper leather seats with little fold out tables, there was enough space to spread out. She tasted her green salad, perfectly dressed with lemon and oil. The grilled salmon and mashed potatoes dish looked divine, but suddenly her stomach turned over.

Oh, no. Not now.

She sipped her sparkling water, hoping for a minor miracle. She *would* keep her lunch down. She wouldn't embarrass herself in front of the sneaky Jessica. But, no. She couldn't eat the salmon. Just the smell of it was enough to have her stomach protesting.

"Gabriel, would you mind if we swapped meals? I think I'd prefer the steak."

He raised an eyebrow and didn't say a word but handed over his plate with eye fillet and asparagus, plus creamy mashed potatoes.

She thanked him and couldn't contain her groan when she tasted the steak. "Oh, this is heavenly. Thank you."

He kept his eyes on her while she ate, and maybe he knew some of what was going through her mind. "Is that better? You were looking a bit washed out."

"Huh. I suppose so. I feel better now that I've eaten."

"Good."

After dinner, he held her hand and quietly kept her company while he read a business magazine, and she did her best not to have an emotional meltdown about the future.

She opened her romance novel and read a couple of chapters, but somehow couldn't keep the story straight in her head. Did the hero really love the heroine? Yes, of course. But would they always be happy? Who could really say? Outside the confines of a book, life happened. Things beyond the heroine's control. Problems, obstacles, all the rigmarole of work and busy schedules, could mean the happy couple drifted apart.

Sinead squeezed Gabriel's hand and wished with all her might, that their love would be eternal. A wish sent out to the universe, awaiting an answer.

Chapter Three

The view from the balcony was incredible – shimmering grey blue sea, palm trees and some kind of silvery eucalyptus bordering a white sand beach, creating a private paradise. Hers and Gabriel's paradise. It wasn't quite sunset here, but clouds would probably block out the colours in the sky tonight.

Sinead leaned over the wooden railing, leaning into the wind. There was a lot of wind. Too much, really. But she was determined to enjoy herself. The almost gale force blasts whipped her hair back from her face and her skin was being sandblasted. But it was all good. *Grand!*

They had a gorgeous suite and they could just hibernate until the weather cleared. She sucked in a cleansing breath and nearly choked on the dust in the air. Still, she didn't want to go inside. Not yet. Not until she worked out what she was going to say.

There had to be an easy way to break life-changing news

to her husband, but for the life of her, Sinead couldn't come up with anything. She tapped her fingers against the railing.

Why was she so worried?

She let out a deep breath. She knew why, if she was honest with herself. Gabriel had a track record of going off on his own and refusing to communicate when his road in life became rocky. When his mother died, Sinead had been beside herself. Gabriel had retreated from her like a turtle pulling his head into his shell.

She'd talk to him. Lay her cards on the table, straight up, no messing around. Well, maybe a little messing around. Would it be so bad if she took her husband to bed before getting down to serious talk?

A click from behind her had her turning, hair whipping around her face.

"Irish, get in here. You'll fly away in that wind." Gabriel spoke to her from the open sliding doors of the balcony. He hadn't ventured outside.

She caught his eye. Oh, he looked tired. Dark smudges had appeared under his eyes, shadowed in the half light. "Okay, show me the room." She reached for his hand and he pulled her close. She stepped forward, aligning their bodies.

"Mmm." She breathed him in, leaning her head on his shoulder. His scent had always drawn her in, making her want to press ever closer. He had that woodsy, but fresh scent that she adored, like raindrops on cedar.

"Tell me what you want to do," he whispered in her ear. His hand settled on her hip. There was a promise of pleasure in his voice, in the way he held her tight.

Sinead wrapped her arms around his neck and pulled his head down until his lips almost met hers. She almost blurted it out. *Almost.* But the news could wait.

"Kiss me," she said on an exhale.

Gabriel was powerless to resist her.

He reached for her face, winding one hand through her hair, meeting her mouth with his own. God, the softness of her, his wife, his love. She was everything to him.

He sank into the kiss, pulling her tighter to his body. She let out a little groan, the kind of noise that drove him wild. He tasted her, breathed her in, the wild jasmine scent of her hair surrounding him. Before he knew it, he'd picked her up so she wrapped her legs around his waist. He broke the kiss for a second to slam the balcony door closed.

He grinned against her neck and whispered, "That's better. Can't let the weather delay us. I'm ready for take-off." That said, he leaned back a little and unzipped the back of her dress, so it sagged down her shoulders. "Take it off."

Sinead pressed her lips together then snorted with laughter anyway. "Aye, Captain."

He stifled a grin as he placed her back on her feet. She smoothed her dress down over her shoulders until it dropped to her waist. Damn, she was stunning. Her black lace bra revealed just enough of her lush breasts to make him want to lick her all over. That was a sound plan.

Sinead shimmied out of the soft dress, and it fell to the floor with a whisper, then she stepped out of it in her little heels. Reaching for her again, he smoothed his hand up one of her thighs until it landed on her nicely rounded butt, covered by a scrap of lace and satin. Grabbing for her like a starving man reaching for food at a buffet.

"Sinead, I need you."

She nodded, looking down his body in that way of hers. Sizing him up. It never failed to get him hotter. "You look like you've achieved lift-off." She palmed him through his jeans.

Damn it, he was so ready, he was about to lose control already. An unholy noise rose from his throat, and all she did was giggle.

"Evil woman."

"Naughty man."

He let out a chuckle. "You're the naughty little flight attendant. You'd better behave. I'm the Captain, after all."

"But I'm not in uniform. Whatever shall we do?" She ran her hands down her body, slipping one bra strap off her shoulder.

He swallowed, hard. "Get in the bathroom. Stand against the wall."

Her lips tipped up at the corners. "Oh, I see. The captain is ready for boarding, is he? Well, I'm nothing if not obliging." Sinead turned and winked at him as she walked away. A classic move of hers that left him helpless.

A choked laugh came up out of nowhere. He was nervous as hell. All his usual confidence was gone. Missing in action. How did she do that to him?

Gabriel followed her into the bathroom, nodding his approval at Sinead standing like a sexy soldier. She blew him a kiss, then unfastened her bra and let it drop to the floor as he watched.

He cleared his throat, then imbued his voice with extra sternness. "Very unprofessional. How are you going to greet customers if you're naked?"

She raised a curved eyebrow. "I thought I could sit on your lap. In the *cock*pit."

With a groan, he stalked towards her, shedding his shirt on the way. "Dammit, Sinead. You'll make me lose my mind."

She reached up on her toes and wrapped her arms around his neck, pushing her perfect breasts against his chest. He took her mouth, tasted her, breathed her in. The wild strawberry tasted of her lips teased his senses as he licked into her mouth, letting her feel how much he wanted her.

When he pulled away, keeping his eyes locked on hers, he didn't miss the way her pupils had dilated. Sinead leaned on him, pressing her face into his shoulder. She mumbled something that sounded like, "Not yet."

Pulling her into another kiss, he made sure she got what she wanted. What they both needed. Connection.

He inched them both towards the bathtub, then paused, waiting for her next move. To make sure the games they played were okay with her. Things between them had been a little weird lately, since they'd both been so busy. They hadn't exactly been ignoring each other, more like ships passing in the night. Or planes in the sky, travelling in different directions. Whatever. He didn't want to stuff this up.

She raised her eyebrow. "Come on, Captain, we're on a tight schedule."

With a nod, he held out his hand in the direction of the tub. "As you say, Ms Kennealy. Follow my directions."

He'd filled up the bathtub earlier while she was outside, making sure it was the perfect temperature. He took off his jeans, gratified to see her eyes widen as she took in the sight. *Going commando, ready for action.*

"Ms Kennealy, remove your underwear," he made his voice convey all the heat coursing through his system. "And get in the tub."

Sinead nodded, keeping silent as she rolled down her underwear and kicked them off. She got into the tub, hopping lightly over the edge, elegant as always. She sighed, moving to sit with her back against the sloped side of the bath.

Climbing over the side of the bathtub, he splashed water over the sides and in her face. She spluttered but then smiled, her eyes lighting up, sparkling with silver glints.

He placed one hand on either side of her shoulders, bracing himself on the edge of the tub. Then he lowered his body down over hers until he settled between her legs, supporting himself with forearms resting along the edge of the bath. It was an uncomfortable position, but worth it for the moan that escaped her lips.

He covered her mouth with his, kissing her long and deep. His arms shook. Blood pounded. She was like summer, sunshine and heat. Lightheaded and short of breath as he was, he still needed more. He'd always need more of her, because she was absolutely perfect for him.

My wife.

Even if one day they were no longer together, he'd always have these memories.

What the hell? Where had that thought come from? She was his wife. He loved her, and she loved him. Nothing was going to pull them apart. Stupid, morbid thoughts. He'd be damned if he'd let his anxiety ruin things between them.

He grabbed one of her hips, urged her to turn over. "Fasten your seatbelt."

Water splashed over the sides of the tub as Sinead landed on hands and knees. She glanced back over her shoulder. "Easy Captain, we're experiencing some turbulence."

He cast his eyes over the length of her body. "Ooof. You're rocking my world. Turbulence is right. But the view? Definitely worth it."

Sinead kneeled back, resting her butt on her heels, shaking with silent laughter.

Shuffling up behind her, he leaned over her and narrowed his eyes. "Nothing to laugh about, this is serious. Brace position."

He eased Sinead over so she rested her head on her folded arms across the edge of the tub, bent over and waiting for him. He kneeled behind her and took in the sight again. She was so beautiful, he could hardly stand it. She'd flipped her damp hair over one shoulder, exposing the creamy skin of her throat. From the long line of her back, to the soft curve of her hips and her gently rounded bottom, she was perfection.

He ran his hands lightly down over her back, enjoying the slippery slide of her wet skin under his touch. And her gentle sigh in response.

Heat washed over him, a surge of need hitting him square in the gut. If he didn't keep this fever for her under control, he wouldn't last long.

She was offering herself but…he froze. It was too much. She was too much.

This needed to be slow and steady, so he could give her everything he had. He wanted to make sure it was the ride of their lives. He wanted to show her, whatever weird vibe was hanging in the air, they had forever. All the time in the world.

Just the two of them.

What was he waiting for?

Sinead had given him the green light. Surely, he understood? She'd agreed to the sexy role-play in the bathtub. She didn't want to waste time. She needed him inside her. To make some more memories, enough to last a lifetime. Just in case.

She didn't want to even think about it, but he might not want to be part of the future that was facing them. When she told him her news, things would change. No doubt. But change in a good way or a bad way? Who could say?

Resting her head heavily on her arms along the edge of the tub, she huffed out a long breath. She twisted her head slightly. He was sitting on his haunches, staring at her with wide eyes. The expression on his face was odd, as if he'd been caught thinking something naughty. She didn't mind a bit of naughtiness, so what was the problem?

Then she saw it – the shimmer of liquid in his eyes, reflecting the harsh lights above the tub. She changed position, facing him fully. She sat and pulled her legs up to her chest, hugging her knees with her arms.

"Gabriel, what's wrong?"

"I... I changed my mind. It's stupid. I need to see your face."

Sinead's breath caught and her heart pinched in her chest. What was he trying to say? He wanted to look into her eyes, to be closer, to make the same type of memories that she wanted. Maybe.

The laughter of the last few minutes evaporated like steam, all the air in the room sucked out with it. She wanted him with her whole self. Her skin felt too tight, every part of her cried out to touch him. And she wanted to comfort him, no matter what was upsetting him. As always.

Her voice caught in her throat. "It's alright. Sit back there. I'll come to you."

She hoped he'd listen, not shy away from her and his own vulnerable side.

Gabriel moved slowly, as if he was walking underwater, not simply sitting back and stretching out his long legs.

Sinead grasped the edge of the tub, then rose so she straddled him. She sat back a little on his thighs, ran her fingertips along his strong jaw, the stubble there rasping against her skin. She kissed his lips, gently, slow and soft. Savouring him. Holding onto his muscular shoulder, she bent and kissed a path down his neck, nipping his jaw. Then on to his chest. His gorgeous, manly slab of a chest. He simply watched her actions, shivering under her touch. One of his large hands was on her hip, holding her in place.

Pulling back, she held his face in her palms and looked directly into his eyes. Some complex emotion sat below the sky-blue surface, a puzzle she couldn't decipher. Like he was asking a silent question. She wasn't sure of the right answer. But she wanted him, with her whole heart.

She stumbled over a crack in her voice. "I can see you now."

"Yes." His eyes blinked slowly, and his lips parted.

Sinead nodded, then looked down his beautiful, hard body – he was hard for her. She touched him, circling him, relishing his shudder under her fingertips. She wasn't waiting any longer. Her fingers trembled as she placed them on his shoulders. Her eyes never left his when she raised herself over him, then brought them together in one smooth motion.

She gasped, her back arching. *Yes*. She gripped his shoulders. A deep groan of pleasure pulsed through her entire body, through both of them, as he reached deep inside, filling her. Pleasure took hold, a formidable force of its own. The rain now falling outside drummed at the hotel's roof, creating a cocoon of sound.

They moved together and a wave of desire washed over her, almost too much to bear. Everything south of the equator tightened. She pressed into him, enjoying the embrace of Gabriel's strong arms wrapped around her back. There was no space for conscious thought, only sensation.

In the distance, far beyond the hotel, the deep bass roll of thunder and the swirling wind, a dramatic soundtrack to the maelstrom of emotions filling her body. Water splashed over the sides of the tub. Her heart thundered. The pulse in her veins kept time, a skittish, scatty beat now. Heat rose in her body, and she kissed him, meeting him stroke for stroke as he thrust into her now.

So close. So good.

Gabriel dipped his head and kissed down her throat, leaving her shivering in the wake of his touch. His lips were so soft. And that hint of stubble, delicious friction.

"So beautiful." His voice was low, a whisper.

Sinead kissed him deeper, tasting him, putting all of herself out there for the taking. No holding back, no regrets. She wanted him to know this was special.

He broke the kiss and shifted beneath her, groaning, as he began to push against her. She gasped when her inner muscles tightened, and a wave of hot pleasure scorched her very bones.

Gabriel moved to caress her breasts with his large hands, circling and teasing the hard peaks of her nipples. One hand drifted lower, sweeping over the curve of her stomach, then he reached the golden curls at the apex of her thighs. He stroked her, smooth and gentle. But driving her wild.

Oh, God. Yes, yes, yes.

The wave of sensation crashed over her with a rush, overwhelming her senses.

"Gabriel!" Her cry, his name, melded together.

She closed her eyes and rode her climax. Then she stilled, holding onto him. Blissful closeness.

Shudders passed through her as Gabriel thrust up into her, gripping her hips. Deep and strong, he moved inside her again and again, then kissed her mouth. He wasn't gentle now. He was ferocious. He claimed her with every movement.

She gasped into his kiss as he tasted and teased her, his tongue tangling with hers. She was so close to the edge again, she could taste it. She groaned as he bit her lower lip.

"Say my name again." More an order than a request. So demanding. It was extremely hot.

"*Gabriel.* Oh, yes."

Her short gasp became something more when he thrust into her, hard. Gabriel's ragged shout of release spurred her on, bringing new pleasure. Breaking waves wracked her system, crash after crash. Then the tide slowly receded.

She fell against him, kissing across his strong shoulder, relishing his warmth and the clean scent of soapy man. His hands still gripped her hips, but he drew soft circles across her skin with his thumbs.

He went still and rested there, and there was nowhere in the world she would have preferred to be. Only with him, in his arms.

This was the moment. She had to tell him. "Gabriel, I have to tell you something important."

"Hmm." He hummed against her neck. He was so relaxed, probably half asleep after all their activity.

She cleared her dry throat. "I'm…pregnant. We're going to have twins, actually."

She felt rather than saw the tension return in his body. He was stiff as a board suddenly, and not in a fun way.

Oh, shite. She'd misjudged this so badly. This was supposed to be a happy moment, but she'd only succeeded in freaking him out. Surely, she could salvage things?

She took a deep breath and blundered on, explaining as best she could. "I'd been feeling queasy for a few weeks. My breasts were sore and I was tired all the time. I thought I'd better have a check up with my doctor, but I didn't want to worry you. She thinks I mis-timed taking my mini-pill some-times, so it didn't work properly." She kept her eyes on him as best she could, but he buried his face in her hair. "I'm only about ten weeks along."

She felt him nod against her neck. Then Gabriel pushed away from her, lifting her off his lap so she sat back further in the bath. Water droplets splashed across her stomach and breasts, chilling her skin, goosebumps rising. She could have wept with the loss of him.

His face had gone slack. If she hazarded a guess, she'd say he was completely shell-shocked.

Her own forehead muscles pinched tight. "What's wrong? That was…special. I didn't mean to just blurt out my news like that."

"Special? Yeah. Sure." His tone was flat and he wouldn't meet her eyes. He nodded, absently.

She stayed silent as he rose from the tub. He was careful stepping onto the wet floor. He slowly moved away from the tub, then sensibly wrapped a towel around his waist. What they'd just done hadn't been careful or sensible. It was mad and wild and everything amazing, but not a good idea for two people who had a secret hanging between them.

She should have known better. She should have talked to him already. She should have made herself be brave, before they even got on the plane for this getaway.

Turning his back to her, he let out a long, ragged breath and ran his hands through his messy hair.

She didn't like his mood change, not one bit. "Gabriel, talk to me. Please."

"It's all good, Irish. All good." He leaned down and placed a chaste kiss on her forehead, then turned and walked straight out of the room without saying another word.

The door clicked shut, and she bit her lip. She stared at the door for what seemed like an hour. Then the sound of the front door of their hotel room closing with a solid *bang*, made her flinch.

She bit her lip.

No. This couldn't be happening. She shivered, feeling all the heat flood out of her body.

"He's left me. Oh, God." Tears streaked her face as she sank back in the bath, closing her eyes on the scene of their lovemaking. And her stupidity.

Chapter Four

"Ryan."

Gabriel leaned on the table in the hotel's bar, blocking out the mind-numbing light jazz music on the sound system. His best friend had picked up the phone, and that was a miracle in itself. Ryan was usually either working or running these days. Pretty much nothing else.

"Hey, mate. What's happening? I thought you were away for the weekend." Gabriel could hear the smile in his friend's voice.

"Yeah, I am. Listen, I have news." He paused to pick up his Scotch in the cut crystal tumbler in front of him, then placed it down again on a leather coaster. "Sinead just told me something huge. I think I had an aneurysm or something. God, I stuffed up. I walked out and she–"

"Hang on, hang on. What's the deal? Explain it to me like I have absolutely no idea what you're talking about, because I don't."

With a swallow of his drink that burned going down, Gabriel winced, then tried to relax enough to think. To retrace his steps. Why was he in the hotel bar and not with his wife?

He shook his head but it didn't really help order his thoughts. "Okay. Sinead and I had been together. Intimately. You know what I mean. Then she blurted out the news that she's pregnant. Having twins for God's sake! I short circuited. I don't know exactly what I said, but I needed some air so I just...left."

"What? Back up a sec. Pregnant? Congratulations, man. That's amazing. And twins, I mean, that's double the blessing, isn't it?"

Gabriel nodded, but of course Ryan couldn't see him. "Yeah. Amazing. You're totally right."

Dead silence from the other end of the phone told him Ryan was processing the other part of what he'd said. Maybe the flat, zombie-like tone of Gabriel's voice was a clue something was wrong, too.

"Mate, did you say you walked out?" Ryan's tone was cautious and calm, like he was trying to talk Gabriel down from a ledge.

He nodded, then ran a hand through his hair. "Yeah. I fucked up. Badly. What should I do?"

There was a pause. "Okay. I'm not an expert on these things, but you two have always been so drawn to each other, and I know you love her. She's supported you through some tough times and she clearly loves you. Use that. Tell her exactly how you feel. Don't hold back. Now is not the time for games. Make it clear you're doing the right thing."

Gabriel nodded again, swirling the Scotch in his glass. "You're right. So, I go find her, and ask her forgiveness."

"Not even that. You're allowed to panic for a second. Explain that you had a mental blip. But be there for her now. Don't let her feel alone. I mean it. When women are pregnant," Ryan paused again, cleared his throat, "they need to feel loved. Safe. Don't let her feel for one minute that you're not with her one hundred percent. Starting right now."

Ryan was totally right. Of course he was, given his own history with his first girlfriend. The difficult pregnancy, then the accident. Losing his girlfriend and the baby, too. The family and the future he thought was his. It had almost broken Ryan. That was the other reason Gabriel had the urge to call his best friend. Ryan needed to be the first one to know the news, to give him time to process it.

Gabriel almost laughed at the trivial thought that now popped into his head. His surprise for Sinead would have to be cancelled. "Oh, and I obviously can't take Sinead to live on an island in the middle of the Pacific Ocean. Not now. Not for a whole year. We'll have to work out what the hell to do about setting up our new resort."

"Don't worry about that now. Seriously. I'll think about it and we'll come up with a plan next week. Go enjoy your time with Sinead."

"Thanks Ry. And I hope. . . I hope you're okay with this."

"Oh, yeah. Don't worry about me either. I'll be fine."

Gabriel ended the call, not entirely believing his friend would be fine. At least, not right away. What had happened in his past had coloured every moment of his best friend's life and changed Ryan completely. He was a loner now, so worried about what the future might hold that he'd chosen not to move forward at all.

Ryan was exactly like Gabriel had been, before he'd met Sinead. Stuck in a rut, so worried about his health and his Mum's, he was going through the motions but unable to enjoy all the good things he had already succeeded in doing in life.

Gabriel had made the call to Ryan, knowing it was the right thing to do, but hating every second of it. Suddenly, it seemed ridiculous to worry about ruining a surprise. He couldn't go through with his plans, not now. There was no way they could live on a remote island in the Pacific for a

year, a place without a hospital. Not with Sinead being pregnant. Let alone having twins.

My God.

He placed his phone on the table, then rested his head in
his hands. The bar was quiet where he sat, all alone. There
weren't a lot of tourists around this weekend except a few
older couples, or so the barman said. Gabriel took a sip of his
drink and winced. He nursed his glass of Scotch that he
didn't really want. He didn't know what he wanted.

Pregnant. With twins!

What an absolute mind fuck that was. He'd never even
thought he would be a father. Never entertained the idea,
until Sinead came into his life. Still, it seemed like a mere
possibility, far in the future. They hadn't really discussed it in
depth, with Sinead pursuing her studies, and his business's
foray into eco resorts. They both had so much on their respec-
tive plates.

And they had just . . . He'd taken her in the bathtub,
rough, not caring about whether he might have hurt her.
She'd seemed to enjoy it, but what if it was a terrible mistake?
Damn it, could you hurt a pregnant woman by being too
rough in bed? Or the bath, as the case may be? Maybe? If so,
he was a first class arsehole.

His phone buzzed on the tabletop. Sinead. He grabbed it
and answered the call immediately.

"Gabriel, where are you?" Her voice shook. Just a tremor,
but he knew she'd been crying. He'd made her cry.

Arse. Hole.

"I'm in the bar downstairs. I'm sorry I left like that. I
needed to process things. I had to call Ryan." Pressing the
phone to his ear, he rose from the table and started walking.
"But that's no excuse for being an arse. I'll be right back
upstairs."

"Don't bother." Sinead was there, in the open doorway of

the bar. Dressed in his oversized t-shirt, leggings and sneakers, she looked younger. Vulnerable. "I found you." A hint of a smile graced her beautiful face.

He shook his head as he crossed the floor to her. "Can we talk? I didn't mean to leave like that."

She nodded, taking his hand. "Let's walk on the beach. It's stopped raining." She seemed okay, mostly.

They crossed the hotel foyer in silence, their footsteps echoing on the marble floor. Chilled jazz still sounded from the speakers overhead and the whole scene was way too calm. His heart beat faster than when he was running around a track. He could hardly think but for Sinead's words spinning around in his mind on a constant loop: *"I'm pregnant."*

She squeezed his hand now as they made it to the wooden boardwalk outside the hotel and walked towards the waterline. It was almost dark now, just a hint of an orangey pink in the sky at the horizon.

Sinead blew out a breath. "I wanted to surprise you, but I see now how wrong that was. I should have told you straight up, no messing around. Getting sex all confused with this news was a mistake."

Gabriel stopped and stared at her, grasping her other hand so both were linked together. "I was the one who bolted. You have nothing to apologise for." He shook his head again. "It was absolutely the last thing I expected. I was ready to tell you about *my* surprise. I had a plan for us to live on an island for a year, in the middle of nowhere. To set up our first eco resort from the ground up. I wanted us to have more time together."

Her mouth popped open on a silent 'O'.

"The first thing that hit me when you told me that we're pregnant, was to tell Ryan I couldn't go ahead with that plan for the resort. And he's my best friend, so I needed to tell him first. But I shouldn't have called him before I even talked to you about it. I know that was a weird reaction. But I needed to tell my best friend because it's the biggest news of my life."

He watched her expression soften, the tension leave her shoulders. "Aye, you're a strange man at times, my love. But did you say *we're* pregnant? You really want this little family with me?"

Ah, shit. What sort of an arsehole was he? The biggest sort. He had to explain, to make it right.

He reached for her face, cradled her cheek in the palm of his hand. "There is nothing in the world I would love more than to make a family with you. If sometimes I act like I don't know what I'm doing, it's because I *definitely* don't know what I'm doing. I never expected this. You. The love of my life."

A tear rolled down Sinead's cheek, glinting in the moonlight. He stepped towards her and wiped the dampness from her cheeks. Then he pulled her close, wrapping his arms around her. She trembled, until he placed his hand in the small of her back. Her breathing changed, slowed.

"I love you, Gabriel. But don't you scare me by running off again."

"Never."

His own heart rate returned to almost normal, then picked up speed again as Sinead snuggled into the crook of his neck, pressing a kiss to his skin. It made him want to throw her over his shoulder and march her straight up to their room. He cupped her jaw and stroked her silky smooth cheek, then pressed his lips to hers. Then, without planning it, he found his right hand cradling the slight curve of her stomach.

"Twins?" He stroked her over the fabric of her leggings. He really wanted to be naked, closer to her. "They're going to be so cute."

Sinead nodded against his neck, then pulled back with a startled look on her face. Her wide eyes had him worried. "Oh, you haven't seen the scans yet! They look so cute already." She moved to walk off, then grabbed his hand and yanked him forward when he just stood and stared at her. "Come on. Upstairs."

His cheek muscles pulled upwards in a grin. "Great minds think alike."

Chapter Five

Sinead sat on the bed and watched the smile spread across Gabriel's cheeks, the real smile, so wide his whole face relaxed and creased up at the same time. His dimples came out in full force. Full of joy. This was the smile she didn't see often enough.

A warm glow like a sunrise spread through her whole body at the thought of a new version of Gabriel she hadn't met before: proud father.

"I can't believe you can already see two distinct little heads."

Gabriel stared at the printed copies of the ultrasound scans, the size of two polaroid photos. He sat on the edge of the bed next to her, turning to show her the same images she'd been staring at that morning.

"It's pretty early, but there's already some evidence they are little humans, not aliens after all." She grinned at him.

He shook his head and snorted. "Good to hear."

Then he met her eyes, and there was an uncertainty in his gaze that she knew well. He was worried. She didn't blame him, not at all. She'd been worried ever since her regular doctor sent her to the specialist obstetrician. Twins could be riskier than single births, but she was still young, she was healthy, with a wonderful doctor, not to mention a caring husband. They would all be okay.

She nodded at the scans, leaned over and took his hand in hers. "So far, everything looks perfect. My new obstetrician recommended another scan at about twelve weeks to check everything is progressing okay. Come with me and you'll see them on the big screen."

"I'd like that, more than anything." He reached for her hand and then pressed the back of her hand to his lips. She loved it when he did that, like an old-fashioned gentleman.

"You know, I freaked out a little back there." He pointed vaguely to the bathroom attached to their suite. "It's nothing to do with how much I want a family with you. I want you to understand, it worries me. I don't know what sort of father I'll be. I didn't have a role model, or any kind of example growing up. It was only Mum and me. I don't want to stuff this up."

She knew in her heart of hearts that was what had been worrying Gabriel. He cared too much, in some ways. He wanted to be perfect at everything he did.

"I'm also having blood tests for my iron levels and all that. So, assuming I'm as healthy as she thought, it should be a routine pregnancy. Even though I might have to eat a lot."

Gabriel grinned and sat back against the leather head-board of the hotel suite's gigantic bed. "I'm not the world's best cook, but I'll learn. I want you eating all good meals, and I'll serve them to you."

She snuggled up beside him at the head of the bed, stretching out her legs. The t-shirt that she wore, rode up her thighs. "Really? I do like the sound of that, Mr Anderson."

His face broke into a sunshiny smile. "I'm glad you approve, Mrs Anderson-Kennealy. Now, onto more pressing matters. I must say, this look suits you." He ran his fingers up her bare leg, stopping somewhere around mid-thigh. He gave her flesh a little squeeze.

"What? Barefoot and pregnant?" She laughed as she wiggled her toes with the dark red polish. Sexy. He raised an eyebrow and made circles on her skin with his index finger. Delicious tingles ran down her legs and back up again.

She'd rid herself of her leggings and only wore Gabriel's old university t-shirt. The one that had been washed a thousand times so it was super soft, but it still smelled like him. It felt like home.

She tipped her head to one side and studied him. "Do you want to go to bed early, husband? I could take this off, if you like." She inched the shirt off one shoulder.

Now, his hand stopped moving. He pulled away and let out a long breath. "Ah, maybe we should get some sleep. You must be tired. No need to take anything off." He glanced away, refusing to look her in the eye.

"You don't think we should get naked?"

"Maybe it's not such a good idea. I didn't know earlier, or I never would have... I might have hurt you. We can't risk it."

"Hmm."

She had heard enough of that nonsense. Gabriel needed to get with the program. Or maybe, she was jumping ahead. Was he really worried about something? Like the way she might look? "Does the thought of my pregnant belly repulse you? Do we need to see a sex therapist?"

"What? No." Gabriel's face creased into a confused frown. Then he sighed, the long, drawn-out sigh of a man about to say something stupid, in her experience. "I only want to make sure I'm not hurting you, or the twins. If we, er, you know . . . exert too much energy."

And there it was. The stupid comment. Ah, well. At least he was trying to be caring. Even if he was being an *eejit*. "That is not a problem. In fact, my doctor said I should try to exercise and keep fit." She beamed at him.

He shook his head and let out a huff of breath. "No, I meant, in the bedroom. Making love."

"Oh, my love, I understand." She grabbed her phone from the bedside table and scrolled until she found the number she was looking for. "Don't worry, we're going to sort this out right now."

"Wait, what are you doing? Sinead? Who are you calling?" His eyes were wide, the liquid blue of the Pacific Ocean in midsummer. Slightly panicked.

Sinead plastered a wide smile on her face and waited as the phone call connected. Gabriel's composure was obviously ruffled, as he sat rubbing a hand through his hair and frowning in that grumpy way he did, when he was all at sea. It made him all the more kissable, not that she'd tell him at that moment. She pressed her lips together to stifle a giggle.

The call connected and the doctor was on the line. Sinead spoke to her while watching Gabriel's reaction. "Hello, Doctor Sharma. I hope I'm not disturbing you too late."

Doctor Sharma replied, "Of course not, I told you to call with any concerns. And call me Alisha."

She flicked her gaze between Gabriel's narrowed eyes and her own belly. Smoothing a hand over the gentle curve there, she remembered something important she meant to ask. "Thanks, Alisha. I wanted to ask, do I really have to give up all coffee and chocolate because I'm pregnant? I heard caffeine is bad for babies, but I might die without any caffeine. Not really, but maybe. Did I mention it keeps me alive? Oh, my husband is here with me. Is it okay if I put you on speaker?"

Alisha laughed, the lighthearted sound endearing her even more to Sinead. She loved having a doctor who was super smart and explained things properly but wasn't a dour lecturing type. "Sure, put me on speaker."

She hit the speaker button and Gabriel sat up straighter and cleared his throat. "Hello, Doctor Sharma. I'm Gabriel

Anderson, Sinead's husband. I'm looking forward to meeting you."

"Alisha, please. Likewise. To answer your question Sinead, some studies suggest caffeine can be dangerous to a foetus, or in this case two foetuses, because it can restrict blood flow to the uterus and placenta. But other studies have shown a small amount of caffeine makes no difference at all. So, I would recommend you limit yourself to one cup of coffee per day and then switch to decaf. Chocolate should be enjoyed in moderation."

"Moderation. Got it. Um, Alisha. There's another reason I called. Actually, Gabriel has a question."

Gabriel shook his head and stared Sinead down. Okay, he was embarrassed. But he needed to know being pregnant didn't mean they couldn't engage in some sexytimes. She pointed at him and nodded, mouthing the words: *ask the question.*

He sighed and finally got the words out. "I just wanted to check whether it's okay to engage in…certain activities." He cleared his throat again. Maybe he was choking on his ego. "Marital relations. When Sinead is pregnant. With twins. I want her to be safe, and I can't even think about hurting her or the babies."

Sinead covered her mouth to stop another burst of giggles. *Marital relations.* Anyone would think he was a Regency era gentleman setting out to woo her over cups of tea in a drawing room, rather than a hot young CEO who picked her up for a one-night stand in a hotel when she was a flight attendant. Or maybe she was the one who had picked him up. Minor details. Anyway, they were a respectable married couple now…happy ever after, *et cetera.*

Gabriel cleared his throat right as the doctor spoke.

"Ah, this is a common concern. I want to reassure you, Mr Anderson, in most cases there is absolutely no reason to avoid having sex or any sort of close personal contact with a pregnant person. But I would caution you both to use your common sense in matters such as bondage and discipline or use of oils and fragranced products that may irritate the mucous membranes. And of course, in the third trimester, things may become a little awkward to manage. A lot of my patients tell me that doggy style or reverse cowgirl positions do the trick."

This time, Sinead let out a loud snort, at exactly the same time that Gabriel chuckled and turned red as a beetroot. It was adorable. Sinead gestured for Gabriel to go ahead and speak.

"Thanks, Alisha. That was very informative. Good advice. Ahem. And please, call me Gabriel."

"Gabriel. Of course. Now, if that will be all, I have to go and check on my own twins. They're three and half and won't go to sleep! But I won't scare you too much with things to come."

Sinead snuggled into Gabriel's shoulder. "Thank you, Alisha. We really appreciate it. Goodnight." She ended the call and chucked her phone down again.

Gabriel's hand snaked down to rest on her thigh and began creeping steadily northwards. "That was truly evil of you. Trying to embarrass me in front of the baby doctor who I haven't even met before." He leaned down and kissed the spot right under her ear that made her shiver.

She stretched out her legs on the bed. "I wasn't even trying to embarrass you. I wanted you to know it's okay to touch me."

"Noted." His hand slid higher, past the point of no return. Because she would not let him stop. In fact, she arched her back, making her breasts thrust forward in his general direction.

Gabriel's eyes flicked up to meet her gaze, and the heat behind that glance stole her breath. He placed one hand over her swollen breast, cupping her. The sensation was so hot, so sweet, it made her gasp. His other hand met the juncture of thigh and abdomen. It only took one more second for him to realise she wasn't wearing any underwear under his giant t-shirt.

With an almighty groan, he leaned down and kissed her, along the top of her thigh, then pushed her thighs apart and circled his tongue, just where she wanted him. Sinead shivered, inching her hips up, just a little. Gabriel pulled back, looking up at her with his shirt bunched up around her waist.

"Minx," he whispered, low and deep.

"Husband."

He raised one eyebrow. "Yes. Wife."

His head dropped, and he was back to work. Working her over. His hand snaked up under the shirt until he palmed her bare breast, tweaking her nipple with his thumb and forefinger. She gasped and ran her hand through his tousled hair.

Sinead squirmed under the dual attack, his tongue between her thighs, fingers massaging, until she couldn't think. She could barely breathe, but she sucked in a lungful of air and gasped, "Wait."

Gabriel stilled, then moved away from her, his hands shaking. "Is everything alright?"

She huffed out a breath but nodded. "I want . . . I need you. Naked. Skin. Come here." She whipped her shirt off over her head in one awkward motion, trapping some long strands of her hair.

Gabriel leaned over her, tearing his own shirt off and throwing it on the floor. Then he smoothed her hair back, kissing her, kissing her, kissing his way down her throat. His hands were on her hip, her breasts, his mouth on one straining nipple. Licking and sucking, he teased her, then groaned louder than ever.

He plumped her swollen flesh with his palm. "Bigger? More rounded? I fucking love this pregnant situation."

Sinead laughed, then swallowed the sound as he moved from one side to the other, between her breasts. "I thought you'd like them. Doc says they might grow a couple more sizes yet."

He groaned again, circling one nipple with his fingertip. "Like them? I'm going to annoy the hell out of you wanting to see them all the time."

"Right, but I need you now. Inside me."

He rolled aside in a blink of an eye. After getting rid of his pants somehow, he was finally, gloriously, naked. He settled between her legs and the hardness of him had her rolling her hips, even before he'd urged her legs wider. His golden skin was hot as the sand on the summer beach, hot enough to scorch. Hot enough to melt. He'd melted her heart, melted her body, time after time.

Gabriel surged into her with a fluid motion, holding himself up on his gorgeous, strong forearms. His lips found the side of her throat, and her heart stopped for a second. Everything low in her body tightened, and the noise they made together was a kind of collective release, a mini explosion before the main event.

Sinead couldn't remember the last time it had been so intense between them. Maybe that first night of the very first day, when they collided in mutual need. It was like that again. Her heart contracted as she heard Gabriel's breath hitch, his body surging. She gripped his shoulders, wrapping her legs around his back. Holding onto him.

Because he was her husband, her heart, her partner in life. The only man she'd ever truly loved. Now they would be so much more.

She squealed as Gabriel reached down and pressed his hand between them, where she was slick and wanting. He stroked her to a fever of thrashing, panting and all together delicious arousal. "Now, Gabriel. Now."

With a final few thrusts, her world coalesced into a single, bright point of light. She threw her head back and gasped, "Gabriel!"

He groaned, "I love you, Irish."

They held each other tight as the warmth, the love, circled them just as Gabriel held Sinead encircled in his strong arms.

"I'm the luckiest man in the world."

She smiled against his skin where she rested on his broad chest. Content. Exhausted. Ever so slightly hungry. Who knew twins demanded so much food? Probably everyone, but never mind. Gabriel would look after her. He'd look after *them.*

Now they were a forever family. And babies made four.

Epilogue

The next day dawned clear and bright, the turquoise waters and golden sand shimmering, as if there had never been any rain. A slate wiped clean, the storm a distant memory. Gabriel yawned into his sweatshirt's sleeve as he jogged along the beach. He had to shake off the tiredness, for Sinead's sake. They had one more day left of this mini break, and he intended to make the most of it.

He stopped by the café in the hotel's foyer on the way back upstairs and grabbed Sinead a breakfast snack of sorts. She'd woken up hungry, as well as nauseous, and he hoped to help her out of her fugue state.

When he entered the room, she was rolled up like a donut in the hotel room's giant bed, wrapped in a blanket he'd thrown over her when he went out. She stirred, stretching, making the cutest little sighing sound. When her eyelids flicked open she spied him hovering by her side of the bed and hit him with an angelic smile. His heart stuttered. So goddamn beautiful.

"Hello, gorgeous." He kissed her lips, lingering when she reached for the back of his head and pressed him towards her.

He broke the kiss to place the brown bag containing her breakfast on the bedside table.

One cheese sandwich on multigrain bread (hard cheddar, none of the soft cheeses for pregnant women), a fruit salad, yoghurt and a large drink in a reusable mug.

"Ooooh, what have we here? Is that coffee?"

"Umm…"

Sinead took a sip from the mug and squinted, her face screwing up in an adorable imitation of an angry pug. Not that he'd mention it. "Is this…juice?"

"Ah, yeah. Combination of mango, melon and guava with some orange and other stuff mixed in. Lots of vitamins and good stuff."

"Oh. Um. Thank you?" She took another wary sip, closing one eye suspiciously.

He laughed, taking a seat on the edge of the bed. "I didn't want to stress you out. We can get a coffee on the way down to the beach if you like."

"Ah, thanks. Now you're talking." She took a bite of her sandwich and blinked at it, as if she'd never seen such a thing before. "Calcium? Vitamins? Are you nesting, Mr Anderson?"

He shook his head, his face heating. "Haha, something like that. I woke up early and read some pregnancy articles online. I want to look after you, Irish."

She nodded, and the combination of the glow of her skin, her cheeky half smile and the way the blanket only half covered her was almost irresistible. She'd have him naked again in no time if he didn't make her get up. Not that he was against naked time. Definitely not. But he wanted to show her something, and they were running short of time.

"Come on, get dressed in your bathers and something on top. I've got a surprise waiting."

He didn't have long to wait, before Sinead was bursting with energy and dressed in the most stunning combination of royal blue bikini and sarong skirt he'd ever seen. Maybe it was the way it emphasised all the newly lush curves of her body, or the way the colour made her eyes stand out. He couldn't stop staring at her.

When they got down to the beach, coffees in hand, Sinead leaned into him and whispered, "Where's my surprise then, you big tease?"

He kissed her cheek and grabbed her hand, leading her along the boardwalk back from the beach, towards a hillside covered in eucalyptus trees. A few cockatoos flew overhead.

They walked for a few minutes, and he was just enjoying the peace and quiet. Walking together, holding his wife's hand. The cool breeze whipped through the trees and sent the white-blonde ends of her hair flying.

"Where are you taking me?" Sinead asked, stopping to lean on a wooden railing along the coastal path. The incline had increased and she was puffing. He hadn't meant to wear her out.

He rested beside her for a moment, then pointed up to the very edge of a white painted balcony and a roofline, visible up ahead through the trees. "There. That house is for sale. I went past this morning on my run."

"And you thought it would be a good investment?"

He leaned into her side and pulled her close. "Yes, but I thought maybe a holiday home for us. It has three bedrooms, plenty of space for kids."

"Oh!" Sinead clapped her hands together. A wide grin stretched across her gorgeous face. "Let's see it."

When they reached the house the agent was waiting, letting them inside for a look around.

Sinead entered first and he waved her through the hallway to the open plan living area. Recycled wooden floorboards gave the place a warm, lived-in feeling, while the sofas and artworks on the walls had a casual, coastal vibe. It felt homey. That's what grabbed him initially, and then...

"The view!" Sinead spun around and took in the almost

three-sixty views through floor to ceiling windows. "Oh, it's stunning."

The beach was below them, waves crashing on the shore and the light hitting the water in such a way, it glowed. But she was the one who was stunning. Because she lit up, her inner beauty shining for all to see.

He turned and watched her then, walking the perimeter of the room, drifting around the space like she was floating, running her fingers lightly over the loveseat by the central windows.

"I can see us here. You and me. The babies. It will be magical."

He kissed the soft curve of her cheek. Whispered so only she could hear, "You're magical. I can't believe you're mine."

Then he opened the balcony doors and led her outside, holding tight to her hand. She gasped, taking in the full view, the freshness of the air, their position in the treetops. It was like a world of their own.

And Gabriel could see it too, stretching out in front of them. A bright future. Everything he'd never known he'd always wanted.

Friday I'm In Love

A Short and Sweet Story

Cassandra O'Leary

"Spank my arse and call me Easy. Is it time?" Jean's startling comment broke the silence in their grey office cubicle.

Megan's mouth popped open. But she shouldn't have been surprised. Jean was often on the wrong side of the line marked 'suitable for work'.

Megan sighed and shook her head at Jean, checking the time on her computer screen as she finished up coding a promotional widget on the online pyjama store's website. Yes, she'd made the animated characters dance in their pyjamas. It was super cute.

She glanced at the clock again. Nearly time. Two minutes until ten o'clock.

Jean rushed over towards the office window, skidding on the highly polished floorboards despite her sensible Hush Puppies with their thick rubber soles. She smoothed back her wild and woolly white locks, flowing free past her shoulders like a mad old hippy, which about summed up Megan's colleague.

"Alright, keep your hair on. He's not back from the gym yet." Megan took a step towards the large windows, casting her eye out the window overlooking bustling and funky Flinders Lane. The cafe crawlers were out in force for their mid-morning hit, but no sign of *him*. "I told you, he's never back before ten. Grab a cuppa."

"No need. I came prepared." Jean lifted her oversized travel mug full of tea.

With a weary head shake, Megan resigned herself to having an audience for her own dodgy behaviour. *Spying.* What sort of a crazy woman had she become? Apparently, the sort who liked to watch big, strapping hunks of Japanese-Aussie beefcake as a side dish to her morning coffee, all from the safety of her office across the road.

All perfectly normal for any twenty-something woman with a healthy dose of hormones but who apparently couldn't get a date to save her life. Not even with a spunky, tattooed ambulance driver who'd accidentally run into her car in the hospital car park last weekend.

The Ambo had called her 'sweetie'. She'd thought a sympathy date was in order. He'd looked down on her five-foot-one inch self, her barely-there curves, eyes roving over her sneakers, baggy jeans and her Pokémon t-shirt. Her face had been naked of makeup, no trace of her usual jet-black liquid eyeliner and no jewellery, not even her diamond stud nose-ring. Her trademark straight and shiny black hair, raked back in a ponytail. She'd looked about fourteen. There were reasons. Like visiting her grandmother and wanting to look respectable. There had been no date.

But today respectable wasn't on the cards. She wore a short red mini dress covered in a delicious strawberry print, knee high pirate boots and enough silver bangles to jingle whenever she walked. Hair, straight, black and swishy. Makeup, on point. *Game on.*

As per usual, she picked up the little tin watering can on the window ledge, which had always reminded her of Aladdin's magic lamp. She gave it a sneaky rub, making a wish, then tipped the can slightly so the water sloshed out the long spout. The office plants needed a dousing, so they'd survive the stinking hot weekend coming up. Her fingertips smoothed along the edge of a curling leaf.

She'd skip the after work drinks tonight in case she got as frazzled. Best to cut out early and get a seat on an air-conditioned train and get back to her flat above the dry cleaners in Nowheresville, outskirts of Melbourne. At least she could sink into a cool bath with a cooler beer. Unwind, de-stress.

Megan stared at her own hands, black nail polish and silver rings gripping that watering can as if it was a life preserver. If only some genie would grant her three wishes.

First on the list would be a decent place to live. Second would be a new job – an interesting job that actually paid good money. Number one and two were inextricably linked, bugger it. A hot date would come third. Or maybe not.

The vision of loveliness in the apartment across the street had her heart palpitating and her knees dissolving. God, how she needed some action. Hot date moving up the charts with a bullet to number one... Sloshing water across her desk, she fell back into her chair.

"Hello, Man Friday." Megan leaned forward, resting her elbows on the edge of the desk, head in her hands. She was like a literal heart-eyes emoji.

God, those muscles entered the room, and it was like she'd stuffed cotton wool balls in her ears. The buzz of office conversation, the burr of photocopiers and click-clack of speedy typing fingers all muffled into white noise. Useless background details.

His was a repeat performance, same bat-time, same bat-channel, every Friday at 10 am, the hunk of burning love unlocked his door, strode across the room and stripped down to his black nylon gym shorts in front of his apartment's floor to ceiling windows. Said apartment just happened to be right opposite her desk, give or take four metres across the laneway and a pane of glass or two. It was a spacious loft full of leather sofas, funky looking lamps, an enormous flatscreen TV and computers. A man cave. Not a feminine knick knack in sight. But that was beside the point.

Right now, the show he put on just for her (so she pretend-ed), that was the point. He peeled off his form fitting white t-shirt, lifting it up, up, and over his head, revealing a ladder of well-defined abs she'd sure like to climb. Tanned skin rolled on for miles, like sand dunes in the desert, making her thirsty.

Was it suddenly hot in here? She licked her parched lips. Her matte lipstick wasn't doing her any favours.

When he pulled the shirt up and over his head, he'd pushed back his damp hair from his glorious face in the process. He rearranged it now, shaking his head. Seriously, it was like rainbows bounced off his cut-crystal cheek bones. His black eyes flashed with lethal intent, or so she imagined. He was probably just hungry.

Jean's wireless keyboard clattered against her desk. "Aww, you could have told me the floorshow already started."

Megan sensed Jean's chair rolling towards hers and scooted to the left a fraction, not letting her eyes leave hottie central. He'd ducked his head below the line of the window ledge, bending to grab his towel from his gym bag. She knew the drill. He'd pop up wrapped in his towel then disappear into his bathroom, stage right.

He popped up alright. *Nekkid*.

No towel, no shorts, no nothing. Well, that was a massive understatement. There was a mighty big *something* right in her line of sight. A sight to behold.

"Hot dog!" Jean shouted, rather louder than was seemly for a woman her age. Not that she cared about stuff like that.

Megan whispered, "Jean, keep it down! I'm busy being inappropriate over here."

The noise ripped out of Jean's throat was full of pent-up longing. "It's okay for you, Megs, all young and nubile. It's been a long time since I've had a package like that marked special delivery to Jean. Or inside my jeans, if you get my meaning."

Megan scrubbed her hands over her now-closed eyes, hoping to dislodge that mental image from her retinas. She opened her eyes again. "Yes, thank you. Now you made me miss... Woah, come to mama."

He'd turned and the view was spectacular. Her Man Friday was as beautiful from behind as he was in full frontal.

Megan grabbed her glass of water and took a sip, just as part one of the show finished. Her Man Friday disappeared into his bathroom. She sighed, turned to her iPad and the graphics she had been working on earlier.

When he emerged twenty minutes later, he wore low-slung black track pants that made him look particularly edible.

He stopped in the middle of the room and stretched, arms to the ceiling, muscles rippling. Then the strangest thing happened. He turned full circle, stopping to look out his apartment window. Directly at her. He raised one eyebrow, then shook his head.

Woah.

It was almost like…he knew she was watching.

FREAKY FRIDAY

Two weeks later, it was Friday morning again. Megan was not on her game. This was despite looking freaking hot. She'd dressed for the sweltering weather in a strapless white mini dress decorated with silver stars, and towering but awesome silver platform sandals.

Three minutes to go. 9.57 a.m. Normally her pre-hottie spying euphoria would've kicked in, but not today. She had a ten o'clock meeting with the auditor, Mr Cruz Ono, or so her online calendar told her. Interesting name, but the meeting was sure to be dull as dishwater seeing as how it had been set up by management.

Dammit! It was sure to go longer than fifteen minutes. She'd miss the whole show.

She downed the last of her latte and slammed down her mug. Time to get moving. She gathered a stack of papers, web analytics reports and the like.

All week there had been coding and widgets a plenty. Nothing she couldn't handle while part of her brain hit the snooze button and rolled over for a nap. Except yesterday, the heads-up came from HR. A corporate re-shuffle was in progress and they were all expected to do the Hokey Pokey. Put their right foot in and shake it all about when the external auditor came to visit. *Ho hum.* He would probably be some nerd come to tell them all about how to increase productivity.

The subversive side of her said she should blab about all the issues. They were expected to run a modern website for a top retail store, an Aussie icon, with last century tools. A content management system that was little better than a cobbled together graphics program mashed up with a word processor. No proper database, no proper training. Here she was with a master's degree in website design and animation like a overqualified monkey with a wrench, tinkering under the hood of a classic car, while she was apparently required to launch a space shuttle into orbit.

She tapped at her keyboard, checking her emails quickly before the meeting. A couple of new messages marked 'Urgent website issue' made her groan. "Oh, no."

"You called?" The deep and throaty male voice with a cheeky note of laughter rang out behind her.

She swivelled in her office chair and nearly swallowed her tongue.

Holy Hottie McHottie, Batman!

The guy from across the laneway. But he said she called him. Did she summon him with her imagination-fuelled lust-powers? Hang on, what did he say?

"What did you say?"

He extended one extremely large hand in her direction. "Cruz Ono. You called out my name. *Oh-no.*"

Megan stared at him blankly. Her brain had left the building.

"Never mind. I'm pleased to meet you. Manny Macauley, the Website Manager, I presume? Sorry to say, I thought you'd be a man judging by your name. And Irish."

She reached out and shook his hand, and *whoa*, didn't that make sparks jump from her fingertips through her whole system. "I am. Irish, I mean. Half-Irish, half-Thai. The parentals are, anyway. I'm all Aussie."

She dropped his hand like a hot potato, though she had the strange urge to kiss it first.

With his left eyebrow raised sky-high, he grinned. Sexily. His teeth sparkled. "Really? Not a man though, obviously." Cruz's gaze took a leisurely cruise of her petite frame from head to toe, lingering on her exposed legs.

She coughed, trying not to have a full-on meltdown. Hottie had looked at her legs! "Bold of you to assume anything about me. But it's Megan, I am indeed a woman, and Manny is just a stupid nickname that should never have been mentioned. Because I'm just one of the guys, apparently." She rolled her eyes.

"Megan. It's a *pleasure* to make your acquaintance."

Did she imagine the emphasis he placed on the word pleasure? Surely not. Hottie McHottie was flirting with her.

Just as she was about to embark on some tentative retaliation flirting, someone came crashing around the corner of the cubicle.

"Holy, Guacamole!"

Oh no. Jean!

Megan's face heated as she turned slowly to her left, checking out a red-faced Jean having a full-on panic attack, while flicking her gaze right to where Cruz was standing. His arms were crossed over his chest, a sardonic half-smile on his face.

Jean sucked in a deep breath and waved her arms in the direction of their visitor. "What the hell… I mean what's our Man Friday doing over here? With his shirt on?"

Megan bit her lip. *Oh no.* But wait, she could still cover their awkward, peeping-tom tracks. "Um, Jean. This *isn't* the underwear model we were waiting on for the photoshoot. This is Mr Ono. The auditor. Come to analyse our IT systems."

Jean's mouth popped open. Her eyes were wide, startled and watering. "Oh hell! I mean, right. Good. As you were." Jean pointed dual finger guns at Cruz, then turned and fled, back to the tea room, probably.

Cruz cleared his throat. The sound resonated somewhere down around Megan's knees.

She nodded at Cruz, who was taking a very close look at her face. Seriously, the way he stared into her eyes, he could have looked right into her soul and seen her guilt sitting there like a lump of coal.

She shook her head. "Right, um, don't worry about my colleague. We should head to the meeting room. Follow me." She stopped to grab her notebook and laptop but didn't worry about anything else.

She couldn't worry about anything else, there was literally no more space in her brain for catastrophes or coincidences.

MEET-CUTE

The meeting went as all these things did. Slowly. Painfully slowly. Cruz had asked about the major projects she had undertaken and the database underpinning the company website.

Megan hadn't had it in her to lie. There was no database but what she had invented on the fly. She'd built the entire website and online store with very little help. She explained about all she'd achieved with basically nothing at her disposal, he nodded and then stared at her for an uncomfortable amount of time. It was probably only a few seconds, but uncomfortable was the word for it. Also, hot.

He was probably deciding whether or not to fire her. Having a full-body tingling reaction to him was probably inappropriate.

Megan tried to inject a bit of levity into the situation. "If I'd known you were coming to rake us over the coals today, I'd have worn my serious intellectual outfit."

Cruz stopped what he was doing, scribbling in his expensive looking notebook. "Really? What would that entail?" His gaze roved over her short white dress, until he blinked slowly and met her eyes again.

She shrugged, acting cool. "My pinstripe dress with matching jacket and horn-rimmed librarian glasses."

He tipped his head to one side. "You wear glasses?"

"No."

Cruz's lips tipped up at the corners, like he was trying not to smile but he didn't quite manage it. "Practical, then. Tell me, Megan, how many staff do you have at your disposal?"

"Full time? One. Just Jean."

Cruz placed his pen down on the dark wood boardroom table with a soft clunk. "One staff member? A website team of two? For a retail pyjama company with an annual turnover of fifty million dollars?"

Megan blew out her breath on a long whistle. "Is it really? Fifty million? That's a lot of PJs."

His eyebrow inched upwards. "You don't seem particularly perturbed if I develop an unfavourable view of the current management of Nora Heart Pyjamas."

She shrugged, unable to maintain even the pretence of caring. "Mr Ono, Cruz, I'll tell it to you straight. My job has been put on the line, no one from management informed me what was going on here today, I'm underpaid and extremely stressed. Now, I have a Boxing Day sale website to create, so if you'll excuse me."

She shut her laptop and rose from the table.

Cruz put a hand on her arm, and she froze. "Wait. Megan, what would you say if I told you I could help? That I'm actually here to help you?"

She bit her lip. His hand was still on her bare arm, a gentle touch but warm as summer sunshine on a sandy beach. "Help me? How?"

"Sit down, Megan." He pulled back his hand, glancing at it before he placed it in his lap. "Please."

She tried not to stare at his lap as she sat down beside him. Their chairs were a regulation distance apart, but somehow he seemed closer now.

"Okay." Her voice cracked on the word.

She sat. Crossed her legs. She thought unsexy thoughts. The smell of the staff fridge after a long weekend power outage... *That did it*. Her belly turned over. Now she totally wasn't thinking about touching Cruz or staring at his mouth. His full lower lip looked slightly damp, as if he'd licked it.

Oh, hell. She was totally staring.

Cruz nodded at her, making his silky-looking black hair flop over his forehead. "I didn't want to alarm you by disclosing why I was here, in advance of this meeting. But, to cut a long story short, I don't just work for Data Core. Our parent company at Global Retail Solutions wants to acquire and run Nora Heart's entire operation. A fifty million dollar clothing business would offer a significant entry to the Australian market."

She sat back in her chair and absorbed that information. GRS was a huge company in the US. They had whole chains of casual wear stores. "Woah. That's big news."

He nodded, his hair flopping again until he pushed it back. "Yes, it is. To be frank, I'm not the corporate boogey man. I wanted to review the IT infrastructure, to report back to my management. We're looking to keep on all valuable staff and grow the business. Now, I think I understand you're running on a shoestring budget, you're under-resourced and underappreciated. Is that correct?"

Megan slicked a rogue strand of her hair back behind her ear. "In a nutshell, yes. So, what happens now? What do you want from me?"

Cruz smiled, the kind of slow, lazy and flirty grin that slid across his face as if it happened automatically, beyond his awareness. "Cutting to the chase. I like that. I like *you*, Megan. What I want… What I'm asking for, is a complete set of records from your little department for the past year. Expenditure, resources, schedules, known issues, website analytics, anything else of relevance. Can you do that for me?"

She swallowed on a dry throat. She'd do that for him, and more. He probably knew it, too. She nodded. "I can do that."

"Excellent. I'll meet you back here at six o'clock. Don't be late."

Wait, what?

She blinked a couple of times. "Six o'clock? Today?"

"That's correct. I have a few more meetings scheduled first, but I'd like to see you later."

The way he said that… Yes, he was definitely flirting. "Right. Um, Six o'clock. I'm looking forward to it. For work-related reasons, obviously."

Cruz laughed, a low, resonant sound that tugged at muscles deep inside she could barely remember possessing.

He sat up straighter, grinning like he'd won something. "Great."

She stood and backed away from the table on shaky legs. It was official. She was flirting with the auditor, who she happened to have a crush on. The man she'd been sneakily spying on for months.

Oh, baby. Jean was going to have an absolute ball with this.

Spilling the tea

Megan flitted around her cubicle, searching desks, bookshelves, drawers and the weird squishy sofa in the corner with a towering pile of reports stacked on it.

She raised her hands to the ceiling. "It must be here somewhere. The reports from the external ad agency. I had them in a blue folder. Where could it be?"

"You mean this blue folder? Under your droopy plant?" Jean pointed at Megan's adorable maidenhair fern on the wide window ledge.

Megan rushed over to the window next to Jean, who was calmly drinking tea from her Garfield mug. Picking up the plant and the file, Megan sighed. "Oh, no. It's damp!"

Jean nodded at her. "So, tell me more about this sexy auditor. He's probably been sent here to kill us, you know. He looks like a spy." Jean sipped her tea. Deceptively calm, she was probably trying to look like she wasn't out to cause trouble.

Megan tried to dry off the blue folder with a tissue from her desk drawer. *Dab, dab, dab.* "What are you talking about? Just because he's sexy, it doesn't mean he's a spy."

"So you admit you think he's sexy."

Megan groaned, leaning her butt on the window ledge. She glanced across at Jean who was busy waggling her eyebrows. "Of course I think so. I wouldn't have been ogling him like a weirdo stalker otherwise."

"Who's a weirdo stalker?" Cruz's annoying, sexy face popped up over the top of their cubicle.

Megan squealed.

Jean gasped and dropped her mug of tea, which didn't

smash, only rolled on the hideous beige rug. Jean bent to pick up her mug, then wandered off, who knew where. She nodded at Cruz on her way past.

Megan had been spattered. Luckily, the tea was almost cold, just the dregs of Jean's cuppa. Megan brushed off the drips from her bare arms and dabbed uselessly with a couple more tissues where brown liquid had splashed on the skirt of her white dress. It was patchy brown now, of course.

She shook her head, making awkward eye contact with Cruz. "Wow, what a day."

"I didn't mean to scare you. Just checking in. Here," Cruz stepped forward into her space, brandishing a white tea towel that Jean had just passed him.

Jean walked past him and threw another towel on the floor, stomped on it to soak up some liquid, then stood and glanced at the two of them in turn. She scuttled away sideways like a crab and disappeared. Again.

Cruz stepped further into Megan's personal space. His scent wafted her way, a spicy combination of something like cinnamon and orange. Like a delicious cake.

He reached out towards her with the tea towel. "Here, let me help."

He sort of hovered near her stomach then…went for it. He patted and dabbed at her midsection until the drops of tea were more a wishy-washy smudge.

Her breath was coming too fast, too shallow. Everywhere his hand made contact her skin overheated, even through the fabric of her dress. His hand pressed against her hip and sparks ignited, everywhere. A weird sensation of falling hit her, her head going woozy, until she literally had to sit.

Megan stepped back and plonked herself on the squishy sofa next to a stack of reports. She looked up at Cruz, hovering nearby with his hand still outstretched and holding the damp towel. "It's fine. I'm fine. Leave it. The dress is probably ruined though."

"Sorry. It's er, a nice dress. You look great in it. I mean, you did." Cruz cleared his throat, and then glanced around her cubicle area. "It seems I interrupted. You should get back to work. I'll see you later."

Then as suddenly as he had appeared, he was gone. Curiouser and curiouser. She'd bet anything that Cruz Ono was flustered by her. By touching her. She pressed her lips together to stop a laugh escaping.

Was it weird to be looking forward to their six o'clock meeting? If so, she was prouder than ever to be an absolute weirdo.

Six O'Clock

It was nearly six o'clock when Jean said something ridiculous. Of course, this wasn't anything new.

"Right, I'm off on my Tinder date." She announced this as if Megan already knew what she was talking about, then rose from her desk and grabbed her handbag.

"What? You're leaving? We haven't finished compiling all the reports!"

Jean sighed, long and low. Leaning on the back of her desk chair, she whispered. "You'll do great. The guy wants to bone you, clear as day. All the UST was getting to me, so I booked a date with a dude from the apps. Must go, getting laid this evening. Priorities, you know."

"Jean!" She shouted at her to come back, but it was no use. Jean grinned her slightly manic grin, then ducked and weaved around Megan to get out of their cubicle.

"Gah!" Screaming seemed like a sensible option, but Megan didn't want to terrify the neighbours in the other cubicles. But now that she thought about it, the office was strangely quiet.

Megan leaned over a partition to glance into the Marketing team's area, and her mouth popped open. *Gone.* Everyone was gone, except one lonely guy at their team's ping pong table, packing up the balls.

"Hey, where did everyone go?" she asked the guy, hoping he could hear her.

He spun around, pocketing ping pong balls as he turned. "Oh, after their interviews with that Ono guy, most of them left. Some are sacked, I reckon. I'm okay, got a new job to go to. Have a good one!"

He waved at her and strolled away, only stopping to grab an entire cookie jar from someone's desk on his way towards the central elevators.

Wow. Megan turned slowly on her heel and took in the silent, deathly state of the office. It really was the end of something. Maybe, it was the start of something too. Didn't Cruz say the new owners wanted to retain the good employees? To grow the business? Maybe it would be a good thing.

Megan scurried back to her desk and started piling her reports into a large cardboard box. Once she'd collected everything, she grabbed her laptop and phone and headed to the boardroom. She glanced at the clock on the wall. 6.15 p.m. She speedwalked across the office.

It was strange there was no-one around. It wasn't usually deserted by the time. At least some of the management team worked later, but come to think of it, she hadn't seen any of them all day.

The next strange thing she noticed, apart from there being not a single person left in the small customer service team, was the smell. Now, it wasn't an unpleasant smell, not at all. A mouth-watering food smell was wafting towards her from the boardroom, and she didn't think it was just Cruz's cologne. It was spicier.

She popped her head around the corner of the doorway to find Cruz sitting at the table, papers and laptop spread out to one side, and an array of takeaway food containers set out in front of him. He also had a couple of beers placed on coasters, a set of chopsticks plus spoons, knives and forks placed on a plate.

Megan cleared her throat and stood in the doorway. "Um, sorry, am I too late for our meeting? I don't want to interrupt your dinner."

He looked over at her and smiled, a half-smile, not so evil this time. "No, it's fine. I was just starving. I didn't have a chance to eat lunch. I bought extra if you want to join me?"

"Oh, sure. That would be nice." Her stomach took that as a cue to rumble, menacingly. She hadn't eaten lunch either.

Cruz laughed, then took a sip of his beer to cover it. He motioned for her to come in. "Come. Sit."

Megan sat and dumped all of her files on the ground, only placing her laptop and phone on the boardroom table. She nodded at the takeaway containers. "What is this, Chinese food?"

"Thai, actually. You mentioned you were half-Thai and it stuck in my brain, I guess. I've been craving Pad Thai all day."

She pressed her lips together to stop herself blurting out, *You were thinking about me!* He was really thinking about food. Instead, she mumbled, "Cool, I love Thai food. Especially from…" she stared at the logo on the noodle box in front of her, "Golden Buddha."

Cruz pointed at her and grinned. "It's the best! You have great taste." He grabbed a fork and opened a noodle box and shoved it towards her. "Here, try this."

Megan took the plastic fork from his hand, feeling the same riot of sparks in her belly as earlier when he'd touched her with the towel. She accepted the box of noodles and dug in, only to groan really inappropriately at the first taste of Pad Thai.

"Oh, wow. This is heaven."

They ate in silence for a couple of minutes but she could feel his eyes on her. Then Cruz offered her a beer. She shrugged, and said, "I don't know if I should. This being a work meeting and everything."

Cruz nodded. "Right. Let's get that out of the way then. I'm currently analysing the responsibilities and productivity of the various teams here at Nora Heart. I was discussing your team's work with the Marketing Manager earlier, and it seems he's very impressed with you. Very."

She tried to hold back another groan, but it slipped out. "Right. Nothing against Peter as a professional, because I think he does a good job. But he's an insistent sort of man. He's asked me out a few too many times for comfort, although I was clear I'm not interested."

His eyes narrowed. "Uh-huh. Do you want to raise it with HR?"

She shook her head, unsure where this conversation was heading. "No, it's fine. I can get along with him if I need to."

Cruz shrugged. "And if he happened to move to the Sydney office?"

Megan went still, except for her eyeballs. She knew her eyes were as wide as the time Jean came into work wearing a crochet halter top with no bra. "He's moving to the Sydney office?"

Cruz shrugged again, one shoulder effortlessly moving up and down with exaggerated loungeness. He was fake-relaxed, she could tell. "I gave him the option of taking a slightly more senior role in Sydney, with moving expenses covered. I think he'd be a good fit for the direct marketing side of the business."

She nodded, thoughts whirring. Peter would be good at that sort of job. He'd also be a fool to turn down what was essentially a promotion. And he'd be out of Megan's way. She wasn't completely deluded. She understood Cruz might be trying to improve her work situation because he fancied her.

That warm, fluttery feeling floated through her and settled in her belly. Cruz was a good guy. Her instincts were rarely wrong about these things. She felt the tug of her cheek muscles, the silly grin that no doubt told him all her thoughts, as plain as if she'd written them on a note and passed it to him under the table. *I like you, A LOT,* she thought at him.

Then, because she absolutely didn't know how to play it cool, she blurted out, "I've seen you before you know. Around."

Cruz met her gaze, his black jewel-like eyes flashing. "I've seen you, too. At the café just down the street."

Megan blinked. "The one with the rockstar barista?"

Cruz leaned forward on the table. "Sam, yeah. He's an old friend of mine from uni. We used to be in a band together."

She stared at him. "So, you're a rockstar, auditor and IT guy?"

He pushed his hair back from his forehead. "Um, I guess. I play guitar but I'm not in a band right now."

She blinked a few more times. "And you've...seen me? Hanging out at the café? Eating their delicious chocolate truffles?"

Cruz nodded, keeping his eyes on hers. She could have sworn his cheeks were turning pink. "Well, yeah. And I've noticed you in the street near here. You're kind of hard to ignore in your little outfits."

What the hell did that mean? Did he think she was a nutter – which was a distinct possibility if he'd seen her in her mini sailor dress with matching hat and pirate boots, or her Pikachu onesie on Wear Your PJs to Work Day – or maybe, did he really like her?

Megan crossed her arms under her boobs. She couldn't help but notice Cruz's eyes tracked the motion.

She sighed. "Are you a weirdo stalker? If so, tell me now so I can call Jean to rescue me from your evil clutches."

He leaned back in his seat and paused for a second before replying. "If you want. But I'm no more stalkery than, say, a peeping tom watching a guy across the street get changed in the privacy of his own apartment."

She placed a hand on her heart, which was squeezing and thumping uncomfortably. She couldn't breathe. She squeaked out, "I'm totally busted, aren't I?"

A slow, slightly dangerous smile crossed Cruz's face. "Totally. But don't worry, I didn't mind."

He rolled up the sleeves of his crisp blue business shirt, exposing very nice, well defined forearms with a dusting of dark hair. Megan's mouth went dry.

Cruz tipped his chin in her direction. "I figured you were watching me for a reason. Either you think I'm hot, or," he smiled evilly again, "you're an assassin who was hired to kill me. I know people generally don't like auditors. Which is it, Megan?"

She squeaked again, "Hotness, obviously."

"Well, then." Cruz raked his gaze over her from head to toe, pausing to admire her awesome platform shoes. He glanced back up and stated, "I'd say we have some things to discuss."

"Really? What things?" She was panicky now. What if he fired her? He probably could.

He continued speaking, over her increasingly loud thoughts. "Dating, et cetera. How does that sound, Megan?"

It sounded pretty good to her. Perfect. But wait, did he mean… "You mean us dating each other, right? Not office policies about dating colleagues and sexual harassment and stuff?"

For a moment, Cruz looked stunned. His mouth was hanging open and his face was kind of slack. "Us, dating, obviously. You're a gorgeous woman, Megan. I like you. And I think it's time we got out of here."

He stood up in one fluid motion, then stretched out his hand towards her.

She took his hand in hers, enjoying the warmth and the buzz of electricity from the contact. There were sparks between them, for sure. She licked her lips and looked up at him through her eyelashes. "Um, where are we going?"

"How about my apartment? It's right across the street, you know."

"Oh, I know."

Cruz grinned, and her heart thudded wildly in response again. Maybe he really didn't mind that she'd been checking him out all those times. Maybe, he'd even enjoyed it. *What a weirdo.*

They headed out of the boardroom, leaving papers and her box of files on the floor. "Don't you want all my reports? That was a lot of work, you know."

"I know. I'll be back on Monday. In fact, I'll probably be working here for some time."

"Really?" She tipped her head to one side and blatantly checked him out, especially the rear view in his perfectly tailored suit pants as he closed and locked the boardroom door. He had a bag of empty takeaway containers and other rubbish in one hand.

He glanced at her, standing just outside the boardroom. "Yeah. I'm looking forward to it. This is a great business, it could just do with a bit more of a plan and some cash in the IT and marketing areas. It'll be a fun project." He adjusted the strap of his laptop case on his shoulder. He smiled again, so a sweet little dimple appeared on his right cheek.

Megan didn't know what to make of this development. The work situation or the dimple. Both were making her stomach all fluttery. "We're going to be working together?

Unless you're planning to fire me. I'm not sure if that's your intention. I'd like to know up front if it is."

He stared at her again, and she was aware of heat rising from her neck to her face. "I don't want to fire you, Megan. I'm going to recommend you be promoted to Head of IT and Multimedia Solutions in an expanded team. I'll be here for a while in a consulting capacity with the new executive team. We won't be working together directly." He cleared his throat. "So, I don't think there's a conflict if we want to see each other, outside of work."

She nodded, several times, far too eagerly. "Good. I mean, the job sounds great. I do want to see you outside of work, too. Like, I really want to. Probably too much, if we're being honest. I've kind of had a crush on you for a while."

He laughed, a deep, throaty sound that had her making fists of her hands by her sides. "I'm glad we're on the same page. Just let me throw out this rubbish and I'll meet you at the elevators."

"Okay, I'm going to get my handbag." She reached out and took his hand again, giving it a gentle squeeze. "See you in a minute."

···

LOCK DOWN

Megan skidded around the corner to the lobby where the elevators were, holding her breath, waiting to see if Cruz was actually there, waiting for her. Unfortunately, he wasn't. Not yet.

She blew out a breath and decided to text Jean. It wouldn't hurt for someone to know she was going to Cruz's apartment.

Jean would be excited about it, rather than thinking she was going off with a serial killer.

She grabbed her phone and tapped out a message:

Hey, guess what? Cruz and I are getting along great! Going over to his apartment now. See you Monday! Megs x

Her phone buzzed just a second later with a reply:

Knew it! About time you had a hot date. My dude Xander says hi. Have fun! Don't do anything Jean wouldn't do…hahaha

The photo Jean attached was of herself drinking a cocktail with a much younger man sitting in her lap, wearing a tank top and backwards baseball cap. He was long and lanky but looked very fit, like a basketball player. Megan smiled. *Good for you, Jean.* She sent back a heart eyes emoji and shoved her phone back in her bag.

She glanced up as Cruz entered the lobby, only holding his laptop bag. He shut the glass door behind him and sidled up to her, stopping a few centimetres from where she stood.

"Hi."

"Hi!" Megan glanced down at her shoes, only to notice how close together their feet were. Her feet in silver sandals, his in shiny black loafers. Their feet looked fancy and super cute together, like their feet were a couple getting married or something.

I am losing it. My brains are toast!

With a sign, Megan shuffled forward to press the down arrow button for the lift. She almost choked when she registered Cruz right behind her, pressing a hand to her lower back.

They waited for the lift. And waited. Megan was enjoying the warmth of Cruz's touch, especially the tingles that radiated out from where his hand slid a little lower to the base of her spine.

She glanced across to Cruz to find him frowning, then he met her gaze. He stepped forward and hit the button a couple of times, but there was no response. The little light at the top of the elevators showed that both cars were on the ground floor. A sudden crunching, grinding noise coming from the nearest lift had them looking at each other again with raised eyebrows.

"Huh. I guess we could take the stairs?" Megan asked, kind of joking. But really, she didn't want to get in the lift when it was making that noise.

Cruz took her hand in his. "Yeah, good idea. I'm dying to get out of here. I have a bottle of wine at my place that we could open."

"Let's go."

They entered the stairwell, Megan swiping her staff card in her wallet to allow them after-hours access. They were on the fourth floor, not too high, but there were still a lot of stairs to manage in heels. She stopped and leaned on the steel banister to remove her shoes, while Cruz let the door slowly close behind them.

Megan led the way down the stairs, keeping up conversation as they went. She got the feeling Cruz was intentionally letting her set the pace. He was a sweetheart.

"Do you think it's a good idea to expand the product range beyond pyjamas?" Cruz asked, as they neared the bottom of the stairs.

"I thought we were done with work for today. But yeah, casual wear would work. I can imagine PJ style pants for working from home, you know, lounge pants. Cute t-shirts and hoodies."

Megan stood at the bottom of the stairs and jiggled the door handle. It didn't budge. She glanced over her shoulder at Cruz, whose frowny face was tenser than before. She jiggled the door handle again, but no luck.

Stepping back, she grabbed her staff card again and swiped the card reader by the door. Obviously, it was after business hours, but that should work. Nothing happened.

"Nope. not opening. What the–"

Cruz stood right behind her and wrapped her in his arms, or reached around her to get to the door. It was cosy. She'd rather he was actually embracing her, not simply trying to get out of the tight space. The door handle moved a little, but the door still didn't open.

Now that she'd been in there a minute, the stairwell was becoming uncomfortable, as the concrete walls and floor created a heat well without air conditioning. It was a disgustingly hot day outside. Sweat trickled down Megan's back, making her feel gross, worn out, and just plain over it.

Cruz leaned in, closer to her body. Whispering in her ear, making her shiver, he asked, "Hey, do you have a phone number for building security? They might need to come and let us out."

She nodded. "Um, good idea."

Megan found her phone and scrolled to find the security number. Sometimes she'd called them when there were building-related problems, like with that elevator that didn't want to work. She pressed the call button on her phone and listened to the ring tone, ringing out.

"I think they must have gone home already. But someone will be on call." She left a brief message, alerting them to the fact that they were stuck in the stairwell, and importantly, the fire door seemed to be broken.

Cruz backed off, and she immediately missed him, which was an odd thought. She watched him turn and take in their surroundings. The dank space was lit by fluorescent security lights that buzzed ominously.

He glanced behind them, back up the stairs. "I'm going back up to check the doors on each floor. Maybe we could get out of here and use the elevators on another level." He nodded at her. "Why don't you keep calling security?"

She nodded, even though she didn't know if that would work. Security would get her message, but if they were offsite it could take a long time for them to get back into the central city. And the other floors probably weren't an option. The elevators were kind of temperamental at the best of times.

Cruz took off before she could say any of that, and she stared after him, even after he jogged up a level and she could no longer see him. She heard the pounding of his footsteps echoing as she placed another couple of calls to security, who still didn't answer. After a while, she heard him stop and bang on a door. It obviously wouldn't open.

On a whim, she texted Jean again.

Hey, Cruz and I are stuck in office stairwell! It's hot and gross. Downstairs door won't open. It's supposed to be a fire exit! If you don't hear from me in an hour, can you call management? I called security already. Thx

Cruz was back a minute later. He was puffing from running all the way up and down the stairs, his hair was damp and falling over his forehead and he'd never looked hotter. Even with a grimace.

"No use. None of the doors will open." He sat down on the bottom step, leaning his head in his hands.

Megan sat down next to him. There was no point worrying about her white dress getting dirty from the concrete step. She was already ruined, at least when it came to cute outfits. She wouldn't mind Cruz ruining her in other ways.

She sighed, louder this time. "I'm so sorry about this. What a stupendously horrible first date I turned out to be."

He looked across at her and grinned. "This wasn't exactly my plan for our first date. But I can't say I mind getting stuck with you." He reached out and stroked a fingertip across her jawline.

Her heart beat stuttered. "Yeah? What were you planning for our first date?"

"Netflix and chill?" He cracked up laughing even as she elbowed him in the ribs.

She sent him a hot glance. "Is that what we should be doing at your apartment right now?"

"I was hoping for something like this…" He leaned closer, until he cupped the back of her head, and she noticed the length of his black velvety eyelashes, fluttering closed. Beautiful. He was a truly beautiful man.

Cruz's lips met hers and the shock of it was enough to leave her gasping. The sweetness of it. The tastes of him, like spice and honey, like something Megan had been longing for but she never knew it. He licked into her mouth and she opened for him, making a sound like a kitten mewling. She tried to pull back, embarrassed, but he just bit her lower lip and groaned.

Well, if he wasn't embarrassed, she wouldn't be either. Shuffling closer to him, she found her hand on his shoulder, the muscles there shifting under her grip. She was holding tight, she didn't want to let go. One of her hands drifted lower, down his back, and then his hand was on her hip, gripping her tight.

The heat of him was a shock – so was his size. She'd been aware of his height, but the strength of the muscles under her hands made her feel delicate, even more petite than she was. So, when he picked her up, actually lifted her by the hips to settle her in his lap, she giggled with the ridiculous feeling of flying.

Cruz whispered under her hair, right near her ear, "Is this all right?"

She nodded, whispering back, "Yes."

He kissed her neck, tasting her skin. He mumbled, "Yeah, so good."

Cruz flicked her hair over her shoulder, baring more of her neck and decolletage, all while continuing his onslaught of kisses. He kissed her collarbone, she sighed. He kissed the edge of her dress's neckline, and she gasped.

Megan squirmed in his lap, letting him go wild. She

wanted it, wanted him. If she was in his apartment right now…suffice to say she'd be wearing a lot less. He'd be naked, obviously, in her best possible scenario.

She was a writhing, panting mess, her lips just reconnecting with Cruz's, when she heard the first bang on the stairwell's outer door. They both froze, staring into each other's eyes. She pulled back a little from their kiss, still breathing heavily.

Someone banged on the door again. The *thud, thud, thud* became a regular, rhythmic beat, then Megan straightened up, listening. She was almost certain she heard someone call her name. It was all a bit muffled, since they were basically sitting in a concrete bunker.

Cruz whispered, "Maybe it's security?"

Megan nodded against Cruz's shoulder and was just about to climb off his lap when a crack of light appeared around the door. Then a drop of rain plopped right onto her forehead.

"Rain?" She looked up, only to get properly sploshed with a shower from above, squirting right in her eyes. "Argh!" She flicked her wet hair out of her face.

She caught Cruz silently laughing, his shoulders shaking. "Sprinklers!" he said, pointing up above their heads.

Megan stood on shaky legs and smoothed down her poor, destroyed dress, then wiped her face with her hands and shook off the drips of water. The sprinklers continued to shower them both, thoroughly soaking Cruz's shirt. It was a good look for him.

Megan's head whipped towards the door as it clicked, then opened a crack, light spilling through the gaps. This time she definitely heard her name. A woman's voice was calling her.

"Jean?"

"Megan! Are you in there?" The door was wrenched open,

and yes, it was Jean standing in the doorway. Bright lights around her blurred her edges, almost like a mirage.

Megan yelled, "Yes! Oh my God! Thanks for coming to help."

She stepped forward and her knees wobbled. Cruz grabbed her by the elbow to steady her. She shot him a grateful smile.

Jean shook her head and glanced at the two of them, who probably looked like drowned rats. Water was still gushing from overhead sprinklers.

"Come on, let's get you out of here," Jean said, as she extended her hand. Megan grabbed it, letting her friend pull her out of the bunker of a stairwell.

Cruz was close behind Megan as they stepped into the building's foyer and blinked at the overdose of light shining on the marble floor tiles. Cruz took her hand and steered her towards his body as they almost collided with someone, just to Jean's left. A huge, lanky someone wearing a baseball cap and a goofy smile.

"Oh, um, this is my friend, Xander." Jean stated this fact with a slight inflection on the word *friend* that maybe only Megan noticed.

Megan smiled up at Xander, who had to be at least six and a half feet tall. "Hi, Xander. Nice to meet you."

When he grinned back, his face creased in such a way that Megan placed his age at closer to thirty-five than twenty-five. Still a lot younger than Jean, but they were both adults, so who was Megan to judge?

Xander shook Cruz's hand, a blokey forearm grip thing that had Megan laughing and Cruz raising his eyebrows.

Xander shook his head, pointing at something to the left of the stairwell door. "When Jeanie said you guys were stuck in the office, I brought my toolkit. But I didn't expect that!"

Megan turned and took in the sight.

A stack of mannequins had been piled up and left right in

front of the fire door, hands and legs everywhere. A dismembered head sat at the bottom of the strange tableau. Next to them, a large trestle table piled high with packaged pyjamas had been set up. A scribbled paper sign read: *Free PJs!*

One mannequin stood tall in a slinky nightie, holding a sign made of part of a cardboard box. The writing scrawled in black marker in the mannequin's hand read: *F.U. Cruz Ono!*

Cruz nudged Megan's shoulder with his and mumbled, "I told you people hate auditors."

Megan glanced sideways at him and met his serious gaze. "I kind of like them. At least, the ones I've met so far."

Cruz took her hand and she stared at him, then almost fell into his eyes, the darkest midnight pools reflecting the lights around them like shimmering stars. The corners of his mouth tipped upwards, and she felt an answering upbeat in her heart rate. Her heart was literally beating out of time, just for him. Who knew she was such a romantic?

He winked at her, conspiratorially. "I like computer nerds called Manny. But to each their own!"

Megan laughed, then turned to Jean. Her friend's eyebrows were high on her forehead, probably wondering if they'd shagged in the stairwell. Megan was sure Jean would demand details on Monday.

"Thanks so much for coming and getting us out. Security hasn't even returned my call yet." Megan tried to give Jean a hug, but her friend awkwardly patted her arm instead.

"No worries. Do you want us to wait for them? You two look like you need a shower." Jean whispered the last part of her statement, but so loudly everyone knew what she was getting at.

Megan stepped forward and hugged Jean with one arm. "You're a good mate."

"Course I am. Have a good night."

Megan grabbed Cruz's free arm. In his other hand he carried two laptop bags and her shoes. She'd help him out, but she desperately needed a change of clothes, and it was like the god of retail walkouts had answered her wishes.

She tugged Cruz towards the trestle table and rummaged until she found a packaged nightie in her size, and some large men's pyjamas that would suit him. When she glanced at him, his forehead was crinkled, adorably.

Megan shrugged. "Don't worry, they're samples. Usually, they go to stores for display, but I don't think anyone will mind if the workers take home a couple of items."

"Hmmm. Whatever you say."

Jean stage-whispered again, "I like him, Megs. He's obedient. And tall."

Megan giggled, suddenly hyper aware of her hand in Cruz's and the way he was caressing the back of her hand with his thumb. "We have to go. Netflix and chill, you know."

Jean's mouth popped open.

Megan waved to Jean and Xander and tugged on Cruz's arm. He was chuckling as they jogged out of the building's foyer, into the smouldering summer heat of the street.

GOODNIGHT

"Megan, do you want a coffee? Or I could make you a sandwich?"

Cruz glanced at her as she emerged from his bathroom. His apartment was only dimly lit by a lamp on his end table, the warm golden glow making the sparsely decorated space cosier. He was standing in the kitchen, looking ridiculously cosy himself in his new PJ tank top and lounge pants that hung dangerously low on his hips.

She laughed as she came closer, and he looked up from the coffee machine he'd been fiddling with, because he was the literal embodiment of a cartoonish double-take. His mouth hung open. His eyes were wide. He looked her up and down in a hungry way, before he could control his movements.

"Wow." He cleared his throat. "You look stunning in that." He gestured vaguely to her body.

Megan laughed, although her mouth had gone dry. "This old thing? Why, thank you." She ran her hands down and over her hips.

Yes, her little stretch nightie was kind of tight and clingy. But the pink polka-dotted fabric was cute, and it suited her. After her shower, the last thing she wanted was to put her damp and destroyed dress back on her clean body.

He'd cleaned up alright too. His two-minute shower just before hers had done wonders for him, let alone her imagination. She'd pictured him in there, under the spray, soap suds on his smooth skin.

Megan crooked her finger at Cruz, tossing her damp hair over her shoulder at the same time. "Come here."

"Yes Ma'am." Cruz marched over to her, maybe putting a little extra swagger in his walk. For some reason, her gaze snagged on his bare feet. They were very sexy feet.

When he was close enough to touch, Megan reached out and placed her hands on his shoulders. She inhaled him, the scent of him, like she couldn't get enough. It was only the truth.

Cruz leaned in and ran his thumb along her cheek, then pressed his lips to hers. For a moment the contact was tentative, silently asking permission. She nodded against his mouth, and she kissed him back, wrapping her arms more firmly around his neck.

Megan's tongue slid against his, and they swayed together in a kind of dance with no music needed. His hands roamed, sliding over the slinky fabric of her nightie, finally grasping her butt.

Cruz pulled away and an embarrassing, needy noise escaped her throat. He smiled, his dimples making her sigh. He walked towards his full-length windows, the ones directly facing her office.

He turned and watched her as he pointed towards the street. "Sorry, but I don't really want an audience tonight. You never know what sort of weirdo stalkers are out there."

She snorted, trying not to giggle like the proverbial manic pixie dreamgirl from a rom-com movie. It was no secret she was a weirdo. But maybe she was exactly his type of weirdo, and he was hers. Wasn't that a wonderful thought?

Cruz drew the blinds shut with a tug on a little rope. "Goodnight, world," he said.

Then he was back in front of her. Only a hand's breadth separated them, but it was too much. She wanted nothing more than to live in his embrace.

Megan threw herself into his arms and they came together like they were inevitable, like nothing could tear them apart. And Cruz kissed her like there was no tomorrow.

Also by Cassandra O'Leary

GIRL ON A PLANE

Praise for Girl on a Plane:

"Cassandra O'Leary's writing is **captivating** and I look forward to reading more from this talented author."

– 5 star, *Readers Favorite* review

"Girl on a Plane is **sassy, sexy and scintillating**."—*Rachel's Random Reads*

"A **sizzling**, emotional read that's perfect for pool, beach or sofa!" – Phillipa Ashley, bestselling UK author

"Fasten your seatbelts. . . Girl on a Plane is a **charming** debut that's sure to fly high." – Amy Andrews, *USA Today* bestselling author

CLIMB ON BOARD . . .

When feisty Irish flight attendant Sinead Kennealy locks eyes with sexy Australian CEO Gabriel Anderson in First Class, sparks fly. But as they jet across the globe from Melbourne to London, it's clear that they're in for a turbulent journey . . .

Stressed-out Gabriel doesn't do relationships. And Sinead isn't about to be fooled by another bad boy after escaping her stalker ex. Then a storm hits, causing the plane to land unexpectedly, and Sinead and Gabriel are thrown together in Singapore.

The pressure rises as Sinead's unhappy past threatens to catch up with her. But might Gabriel be the one to heal her heartbreak? If he could open up about his troubling secrets, maybe a relationship could actually get off the ground. Fasten your seatbelts – this WON'T be a smooth ride . . .

Available now in ebook – books2read.com/GirlOnAPlane

HEART NOTE

A Christmas Romcom Novella

A laugh out loud Christmas novella, perfect for fans of Love Actually . . .

It's almost Christmas, the department store is bedecked with baubles and Lily has about eleventy billion gifts to wrap and sell. She and her team of spritzer chicks are glamorous, professional and hoping they don't have to wear the hideous red onesies and reindeer antlers the store manager has in mind.

The high point of Lily's work life is Christos Cyriakos, ex-cop, security guard, possible Greek god. He's a mystery box she'd love to unwrap. But can she trust him? All Lily wants for Christmas is to kiss Christos (and more), catch a band of thieves running amok in the store, and live happily ever after. Is that too much to wish for?

Available now in ebook and paperback – books2read.com/HeartNote

Coming soon… Late 2022 release

DATING LITTLE MISS PERFECT

The perfect read for fans of *The Soulmate Equation* by Christina Lauren and *The Hating Game* by Sally Thorne…

On an anonymous online dating app, LittleMissPerfect meets HotAussie007 and it's love, or lust, at first click. In real life, a smart but spiky STEM heroine (research scientist, Dr Eden) meets a laid-back Aussie (marketing manager, Finn) at the big pharma company where they both work in California.

When they realise the truth about their online alter egos, dating is off the table. Can they ignore their inconvenient attraction, and work together to take down their unethical boss? Or will intense rivalry cause their IRL work lives and online love lives to collide and explode like a science experiment gone wrong?

Visit Cassandra's website for more news:

cassandraolearyauthor.com

Read on with a sample of Cassandra's debut novel, *Girl on a Plane*. Copyright Cassandra O'Leary 2016.

GIRL ON A PLANE

Mermaid Airlines Flight 180, Melbourne to London

Showtime! Sinead Kennealy sucked in a deep breath and squared her shoulders. Time to get it over and done with. The molly-coddled first class passengers wouldn't entertain themselves, apparently.

She sensed her colleagues Yuki and Deanna on either side of her usual position, centre front of the cabin. Yuki flicked her shiny black ponytail over her shoulder and flipped on the PA system. The airline's theme song, a hackneyed rendition of the "Macarena", blared from the plane's speakers.

Hey! Mermaid Airlines.

Sinead's heart sank like a stone dropped in a bucket of water even as she plastered on the airline's trademark happy smile. Her jaw ached with the enforced perkiness, all day long. It was only breakfast time and she had a crick in her neck. A few more hours and they'd land in Dubai. She might have time for a massage at the hotel spa.

She shimmied forward in a practised and synchronised routine. The move she hated. The booby shake. A couple of mature men eagerly watched her from their premium seats with an over-excited gleam in their eyes.

One of the men mumbled, "Shake it, baby!"

Heat crawled up her throat to her cheeks and she wanted to slink away to the bathroom. Surely she couldn't die from embarrassment. But it was a close call.

How much more of this job could she take? As an eager twenty-one-year-old recruit with Mermaid Airlines (*The funnest airline in the world!* So the tag-line went) she'd been bouncing off the walls with glee. The travel! The glamour! The most exciting job ever. Five years on, either her patience had run out or her expectations had grown.

Shimmy, shimmy, shake!

She kicked her leg. Shook her hips. A grown woman. Fluent in French, German and English, plus a sprinkling of Gaelic. A first-aid expert. Calm in an emergency. She had some mad skills these days. She'd even talked down an over-zealous pilot keen to initiate her into the Mile High Club. But look at her shaking her money-maker. Was it too much to ask for something more challenging?

Shimmy, shimmy, kick!

While she was ranting, why didn't her male colleagues ever have to shake their tails to keep the high-flying passengers happy? Fecking Damian smirked at her over the passengers' heads, from the rear of the cabin. Skiving off again. She gave him the evil eye, a slight pinch of her eyebrows the passengers wouldn't notice. But he sure noticed, and scurried away like a little mouse back to the galley where he was meant to be preparing breakfast. She'd deal with him later.

Shimmy, kick!

She bowed. Enthusiastic applause from the whole cabin drowned out the roaring engines as the music died. She grabbed the microphone from Yuki.

"Thanks ladies and gentlemen. Welcome to Mermaid Airlines flight 180 from Melbourne to London via Dubai. We will be serving breakfast shortly. In the meantime, please watch this short safety video."

Mirroring the gestures in the safety video, she pointed out the nearest exits. Her arms went off on their own merry way, demonstrating on auto-pilot. A yawn rose up in her throat. So tired. She could have shut her eyes and slept where she stood. But her lips stretched upwards, and she nodded at the passengers in front of her.

A mixed bunch today. Business people mostly. One younger man in dark glasses who might have been a football player. Yuki would know, she was always up to speed on celebrities. Older Aussie gentleman in 5K, already showing signs of downing too many beers in the airport bar. And it was only eight o'clock in the morning. The heckler. She'd keep her eye on him.

She held up the airline's safety card and waved in the direction of the oxygen masks.

A couple of other passengers stood out. Young professional-looking mother in 16G, dressed all in black, travelling alone with her baby. Was she wearing a Chanel suit? A different world, these rich people lived in. Who wore Chanel when they travelled? Let alone when they'd likely be covered in baby vomit in no time at all?

No matter, the bub was bound to annoy the first and business travellers. She'd help out by holding the baby when Mummy needed to go to the bathroom. He looked a sweet little thing. The random baby cuddles were a definite perk of the job.

She glanced towards Deanna. Her friend was well into robot mode, her dark eyes bright and blank.

Sinead scanned the rest of her passengers, letting her gaze slide over the business people who all looked much the same. Except…

Well, hello there.

Shockingly handsome young man with a perfectly sculpted face, full, kissable lips, sparkling blue eyes and dark blonde hair in 3A. Her belly fluttered and flipped. She was experiencing mild turbulence. Because of him? Her gaze tracked down his long, lean form, from broad shoulders to slim hips under a sharply cut suit. The man knew how to wear a suit.

And the man stared directly at her with intent—anyone would think he wanted to pounce on her and eat her alive. Yowza. Her stomach performed its own little dance and flipped over in the most peculiar way. As if she was falling.

Her hands formed into fists at her side and she sucked in a soothing deep breath. She was all hot then cold, goosebumps pebbling down her arms. The last thing she needed was another man who wanted to own her. But not all muscular and fit men were like Padraig. She'd left her mad ex-boyfriend years and thousands of miles away. Why couldn't he stay there, out of sight, out of mind?

Don't engage the crazy. Calm blue ocean. The image of a tropical Thai beach popped into her mind and calm washed over her like gentle waves against the shore.

She was still staring at Mr Hot Stuff in 3A. Rubbing her arms, she hastily looked away.

It was nearly time for the coffee and tea service, not the time for the distraction of a handsome man with a James Bond-ish air about him. Who looked like he would be able to handle himself… and a woman too.

What would it feel like, to let him handle her? Oh, Lord. She had a sneaking suspicion it would feel mighty fine. Heat crept up her throat and surged across her cheeks. The last thing she needed was a blush lighting up her face like an emergency beacon.

She lowered her arms and finished up the safety demo. And stood there staring for a few seconds too long. She'd better catch up to Yuki and get the beverage cart stocked. Time to crack on.

Gabriel cocked his head to one side and stared as her skin changed from pale porcelain to hot pink. The platinum blonde flight attendant was having some kind of reaction to him. Damned if he could tell whether it was good or bad.

He gripped the iPad tighter in one hand where it balanced on his lap, as her red glossy mouth popped open and she inhaled deeply.

He'd first noticed her at the boarding gate, walking away from him towards the large wall of windows overlooking the runway. Her body had been framed in silhouette—the outline of long, slim legs and a shapely backside in her tight skirt drew his gaze and fired his imagination.

She seemed so confident and in control, a woman to be reckoned with. It had been a while since he met a sexy woman who wasn't a complete pushover. Someone to spar with. He let the idea percolate as she headed off towards the staff area, behind the curtain at the front of the plane. The sway of her hips as she walked down the aisle was definitely some of the best inflight entertainment he'd seen in a long time.

He stopped gawking and let his gaze drop to his iPad and the designs for his company's new travel blog. Something was off with the style but he couldn't put his finger on it. The main Global Village website was doing fantastic business, especially since his deal with the major airlines flying through the Asian region.

But the demands from the board and shareholders were taking a toll. He rubbed his right temple with his forefinger, tiny circles, round and round. There was pressure to expand the business too quickly, pressure to push into new markets, and the constant pressure to make more money.

He'd commissioned a cutting-edge digital advertising agency to develop the new Asia blog. But they weren't getting it right. What the hell was going on? He'd have to step in. Talk to the designers, get them to start from scratch. As if he didn't have enough on his to-do list.

It was so hard to let go.

After starting a business fresh out of university and building it into a global brand, it wasn't so easy to hand over the reins. Now the business was expanding from his home city of Melbourne to London. He should have stepped back and allowed the new Europe and Asia-Pacific regional managers to do their jobs. Instead he was on a flight to London to supervise the set-up phase for the new office.

He wasn't sure he should have left his Mum, even if it was only two weeks. He'd promised to always be there for her. The guilt and stress threatened to devour him if he let it take over. He pushed it down till his gut ached. He needed a break. Some downtime to decompress.

It had been so long since he went on a proper holiday. Gabriel pictured the top of the range surfboard stashed somewhere in his Mum's house. He'd love to take off surfing and drop-out for a while. Not likely in sunny London in February. He could try to take a weekend trip to Spain or down the coast back home. Surfing was the only personal time he seemed to get these days.

The other flight attendant pushed the drinks cart down the aisle and stopped beside his seat. She was pretty with her black glossy hair and even blacker eyes. Wide eyes. She looked younger than the other hostess. Yuki, he read on her name tag. He'd have a bit of fun with her, cheer himself up. He liked to flirt, hopefully she'd be into it too.

"Coffee or tea this morning?" Yuki asked.

"Let's see. Is the coffee likely to be any good? On a scale from one to ten—one being sludge scraped off the bottom of the Yarra River to ten being nectar of the gods—how would you rate it, Yuki?"

She blinked, pausing for a second. "Ah, I believe the coffee is good, Sir. Would you like a cup?"

He raised his eyebrow. She was no fun. "You didn't answer my question. If you give it a six or higher I'll try it."

"Right. I'd give it a six or seven." Yuki poured the cup of coffee and set it on a small plastic tray, ready to pass across to him. He waved it away

The tall blonde approached behind Yuki to help with the drinks service. His eyes instantly snapped to hers and then his gaze moved lower, to the name tag pinned above her perfectly round, high breasts. Wicked thoughts flitted through his mind, which she could obviously read in his expression. A pinched crease formed between her eyebrows, then her tongue darted out and licked across her soft-looking lower lip. Half-annoyed, half-interested?

Sinead. He noted her name in his memory bank. She had a musical Irish lilt in her accent when she'd made the announcement over the PA. Very sexy.

"Can I be of assistance?" Sinead's voice was a little husky. Very sexy indeed.

Yuki nodded to Sinead and stepped past her, continuing to serve the next passenger.

"I was asking Yuki whether the coffee was any good. What do you think, Sinead?"

"Well, it's hardly Jamaican Blue Mountain, but it'll do in a pinch." She winked at him, actually winked.

He liked this woman. His mouth tugged up at the corners. Too long. It'd been too long since he'd met a woman he wanted to banter with.

"You know all about Jamaican Blue Mountain coffee, do you?"

The condescending comment was out of his mouth before he could stop it. Scorn dripping off his tongue seemed to be his default setting when talking to women lately. Too much time spent with his Mum, nurses, doctors, all women telling him things he didn't want to know. He had to snap out of it. Charm came easily when he tried. He hadn't always been a grumpy bastard.

Her lips twitched and she leaned a little lower over his seat. "As it happens, I do. Blue Mountain coffee beans come from a tightly controlled region in Jamaica and are considered the best in the world by many critics. We don't currently stock it on board, but I can recommend a few excellent cafés in London serving it, for when you arrive."

"Really? Do tell."

"There is Tomtom in Belgravia of course, but my personal favourite is Nude Espresso in Soho Square."

"Nude Espresso?" Gabriel raised his eyebrows. Was she flirting with him? Things were looking up.

"Yes. Nude." Sinead's cheeky half smile answered the question.

Hello, Irish fling. Definite interest there.

He chuckled, stretching out his legs. "Hmm, I'll keep it in mind. But right now I'll take a pot of tea."

"Of course you will. Sir." Sinead muttered the last word, reaching for the tea on her cart. The frown crossing her face was a kick in the guts, before she beamed like a little ray of sunshine.

He should've known better. In her mind, he was nothing but another rich arsehole, and she was used to serving them without a second glance. Unless he could show her he was different.

He wanted to be different. He didn't want to be a man who would ruin a woman's day. He'd like to make Sinead smile. Now wasn't that a surprise?

Buy *Girl on a Plane* now to continue reading –
cassandraolearyauthor.com/books

Acknowledgments

Thanks to my superhero husband and my kiddos, the mini ninjas. Love you, guys! But please, keep the noise down!

A huge thank you goes to the members of my fabulous writing group, the Melbourne Romance Writers Guild. *Chocolate Truffle Kiss* was first published in *Sweet and Spicy – A Celebration of Romance*, an anthology written by members to celebrate the group's 25th anniversary year in 2015. *Tree Love* was first published in the *Taste of Romance* anthology in 2017, also published by the group. I've come a long way since my first stories were published, but my newer work owes everything to the things I learned as a member of the group.

My writer friends including Michelle Somers, PJ Vye, Savannah Blaize, Samara Parish and Lauren Harbor have been *amazingly amazing*, at all times! PJ Vye especially has helped with feedback and formatting the print edition of this collection. What a star!

I'd also like to thank the Romance Writers of Australia, an awesome-sauce association of writers who introduced me to the whole concept of romance writing in all its forms, sub-genres and publishing options. They taught me how to become a published romance author in Australia from go to woah. While my road to publishing has been winding and sometimes convoluted, involving competitions, traditional publishing, self-publishing, group publishing, submissions to agents and applying for grants, I have appreciated the camaraderie and support of this organisation at every stage.

My gratitude also goes to Creative Victoria and Regional

Arts Victoria, for creating a special grants scheme for creative workers affected by COVID-19 and all the associated lockdowns and hardships involved in the period from 2020 to 2021. Producing this story collection is just one of the projects I have been able to complete, since receiving a grant in December 2021.

Last but definitely not least, thank you to all my wonderful readers. I know some of you have been waiting for paperback versions of my work, so I hope you enjoy this collection. I promise there will be more to come! Try and stop me!

About Cassandra O'Leary

Cassandra O'Leary is an author, freelance writer, avid reader, corporate communications escapee and admirer of pretty, shiny things! In 2015, Cassandra won the global We Heart New Talent contest run by HarperCollins UK, and her debut romantic comedy novel, *Girl on a Plane*, was then published in 2016. She was also nominated for the AusRom Today Reader's Choice Award for Best New Author. More recently, Cassandra has independently published novellas and short stories, all while hanging out with her superhero husband and chasing her two mini ninjas around her home city of Melbourne, Australia. She loves/hates writing multiple things at once, and she has several more novels in the works. Cassandra is a proud member of Romance Writers of Australia and the Melbourne Romance Writers Guild.

Read more at **cassandraolearyauthor.com** and sign-up for newsletter updates!

Follow Cassandra O'Leary on social media
   Facebook – www.facebook.com/cassandraolearyauthor

Instagram – www.instagram.com/cassandissima
Twitter – www.twitter.com/cass_oleary